"First wrong choice is to start to scream, lady,"

Edge told her evenly. "You'll drown in your own blood from a cut throat before you finish it. Second one is to act the dumb blonde so I have to put the pressure on you. Best to tell me what I need to know and that way your headache won't get any worse."

"Please, mister," she hissed through her gritted teeth, and then closed her eyes tightly. "You murdered the man I was going to marry. Frank's dead so there's nothing you can do to cause him more harm. And I can't understand. Why do you want to cause me more suffering than you have by shooting him down like some mad dog you'd cornered in a—"

"Okay, lady. The way you dress for bed I couldn't help but see you ain't a true blonde. And I've heard enough to know you're not dumb. All you have to—"

"This is crazy. Like a nightmare. My whole world is getting turned upside down." There was a tremulous shrillness in her voice and her eyes began to emanate a hard glitter as she moved toward hysteria . . .

Other titles in the **EDGE** series from Pinnacle Books

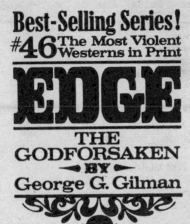

Best-Selling Series!

#46 The Most Violent
Westerns in Print

EDGE

THE GODFORSAKEN

BY

George G. Gilman

PINNACLE BOOKS NEW YORK

This is a work of fiction. All the characters and events portrayed in this book are fictional, and any resemblance to real people or incidents is purely coincidental.

EDGE #46: THE GODFORSAKEN

A Pinnacle Books edition, first published in Great Britain by New English Library.

New English Library edition / March 1984
Pinnacle edition / August 1984

ISBN: 0-523-42265-2

Cover art by Bruce Minney

Printed in the United States of America

PINNACLE BOOKS, INC.
1430 Broadway
New York, New York 10018

9 8 7 6 5 4 3 2 1

For R.P.
the out-of-town money man.

About The Author

George G. Gilman was born in 1936 in what was then a small village east of London; he attended local schools until the age of fifteen. Upon leaving school he abandoned all earlier ambitions and decided to become a professional writer, with strong leanings toward the mystery novel. He wrote short stories and books during evenings, lunch hours, on weekends, and on the time of various bosses while he worked for an international news agency, a film company, a weekly book-trade magazine and the Royal Air Force.

His first short (love) story was published when he was sixteen and the first (mystery) novel appeared ten years later. He has been a full-time writer since 1970, writing mostly Westerns, which have been translated into a dozen languages and have sold in excess of 15 million copies. He is married, has a dog and lives on the Dorset coast, which is as far west as he intends to move right now.

Chapter One

THE big Texas sky was featured only by the glaringly bright and blistering hot noon sun. The twin rails of the single-track Prospect and North Texas Railroad cut a gleaming arc across the red and brown and gray and green country of rolling hills, rearing outcrops and meandering dry washes under this pale blue sky with the dazzling daub of yellow.

At this hottest time of the day, work perhaps slackened but did not stop on the building that was being constructed a short way to the west of the railroad track, in a supplies-littered area bounded on the other three sides by a cluster of wickiups, a strangely eroded outcrop of gray rock, and a campsite comprised of an elderly covered wagon, a remuda of team horses and Indian ponies and a collection of actual and improvised furniture. A fire was burning in a circle of stones, and a blackened cooking pot suspended in the flames from a tripod of irons was giving off aromatic steam that almost masked the acrid taint of the burning cordwood.

Norah Loring was dividing her attention between the fire and the vegetable stew cooking over its heat and a darning chore as she sat on a rocking chair in the sparse midday shade of the wagon's side. She was additionally shaded by a large hat that was as worn and as unfashionable as her dress and her boots. But, despite the drab colors and lack of style about her clothing, she could not fail to be what she was: a fine-looking woman who had not yet reached the prime of her life. She was, in fact, just twenty-three years of age, and the bloom of youth was in the process of fading as the far more attractive signs of blossoming womanhood began to replace it. This in the prominence of her delicate facial bone structure beneath her pale, unblemished skin; the way in which the innate knowledge of her kind was subtly hinted at by an odd lightness that occasionally glinted in the depths of her gray eyes; and even in the set of her not quite full lips when she smiled at a secret thought that once would have caused her to blush.

This pretty face on the brink of becoming beautiful was framed by thick, shoulder-length, naturally curled hair that was colored somewhere between blonde and auburn. Appropriately, her body and limbs were adequately concealed by the high-necked, low-hemlined and long-sleeved dress. But on those occasions when she rose from the rocker and moved the few paces to attend to the fire or the contents of the cooking pot, it was easy to see that she was a slender but certainly not thin woman: alluringly proportioned for her height of more than five and a half feet.

When she was finished with the darning of her husband's black frock coat, she set aside the garment and the needle and thread on a nearby up-ended crate and gazed adoringly across at where Austin was working with the Indians on the small chapel. Working not as hard nor as fast as any of the five Apaches, four Comanches and the lone Cheyenne, perhaps—because he was more than twice the age of the oldest brave—but with a greater degree of enthusiasm for the labor than any of the younger men. This seen in the quiet smile that permanently wreathed his sweat-run face and the slow deliberation with which he finished each task to his own satisfaction before he moved on to the next; while at the same time he maintained a cautious but beneficent watch over the braves engaged on the more arduous work.

Not that the Indians were unhappy as they strained and sweated and even perhaps sometimes cursed in their native tongues as they toiled in the draining heat of the high sun. They grinned and laughed and traded an almost constant stream of badinage amongst themselves. And occasionally they made goodnatured fun of Austin, although they always paid close attention to his instructions and the tactful criticisms which he issued from time to time: did their best to do what he asked of them.

But the stripped-to-the-waist braves, some wearing breechclouts of rawhide while others wore native-made hide or store-bought denim pants, enjoyed the chores simply because they knew they were pleasing the Reverend Austin Henry Loring by helping their friend and benefactor to build his chapel beside the rock of Jesus. Whereas the minister, attired in black boots, pants, shirt with a white cleric's collar and a wide-brimmed, low-crowned hat of gray with a black band, derived his brand of profound and serene contentment from the sure and certain knowledge that he was doing God's will: harbored the conviction that never before during the more than twenty years since he was ordained a Baptist minister had he served the Almighty to the complete satisfaction of the Lord until he began to build this chapel.

This was what Austin had told his wife in the night after the day he had dug the first shovelful of dirt that started the construction of the timber and adobe building on the sagebrush-choked, stone-littered, rock-hard acre or so of ground between the tracks and the fifty-feet-high limestone outcrop. That had been less than eight weeks earlier and in that time, to Austin's way of thinking, a great deal had been achieved. Two sides and the rear wall of stark white adobe were up and three-quarters of this single-story area had been flat-roofed with timber. And the as yet unglazed arched frames of the side and rear west windows were in position. Now Austin and his band of inexpert but cheerfully willing helpers were preparing to start work on the belfry tower which was planned to rise more than twice as high as the rest of the chapel at the east front of the building.

As Norah rose again from the rocker and went to stir the bubbling stew, she resisted the urge to shake her head in covert admiration of her husband's forbearance. To her way of thinking, much more should have been achieved toward the completion of the chapel since they had arrived aboard the wagon and watched the off-loading of the building supplies from the freight cars. But just the Cheyenne brave arrived on the appointed day. Two of the Apaches came a week later and the other three and one of the Comanches more than a week after that. The final trio of Comanches did not put in an appearance until ten days ago. Whereas if they had all been here at the time they promised, their wickiups built and . . .

She glanced toward her husband once more and halted her train of thought with a sigh, yet again resigning herself to what was undeniable—that this man could not be judged by the yardsticks that were normally applied to others. Even when he was not attired in his clerical garb and engaged in obvious spiritual pursuits, in her view Austin always looked and acted every inch a man of the cloth. And, as his wife, she had seen him totally naked and overflowing with sexual passion which he released into her own brazenly nude body. Now, as this image came unbidden into her mind, she experienced a tremor of excitement. Then she felt her cheeks flush when her husband seemed to sense her secret thoughts and looked toward her—

his fleetingly wicked smile suggesting that his own mind had been host to a notion not dissimilar to that which disturbed her. And then he winked, so that she could be entirely sure again, if she was in need of such reassurance, that his divine love of God was not so totally fulfilling that he would ever neglect to love her with every temporal fiber of his body. And Norah grinned, almost laughed aloud, as she marveled at the extent of what could be tacitly transmitted by the swiftest and simplest of signs between two people so deeply in love with each other.

Then she returned to the unnecessary task of stirring the stew, and Austin continued with measuring and marking the planks of timber from which two of the Indians were making the door of the chapel. The husband once more entirely concerned with doing the will of God, the wife reflecting on how that knowing and close to salacious wink by a man of such profound religious beliefs served to speak volumes about the kind of person he was.

Austin Loring was not a physically striking man. Standing a little less than six feet tall in his boots, he had a slender and even frail-looking build: weighed not much more than a hundred and fifty pounds with little variation between the girth of his chest, his waist and his hips. Because he was so thin, his arms and legs seemed to be overlong. His features were gaunt, with jutting brows, prominent cheekbones, pointed nose and sharp jaw; and at times, when he was morose, his face could resemble the death mask of a man who died from a

wasting disease. But, invariably, there was a bright-
ness in his deep-set blue eyes and a cast to the line
of his mouth that left no doubt he was a man full
of life and eager to have others share his delight in
the pleasure of simply being alive. He had a head
of strong-growing gray hair and his wrinkled and
weather-burnished face was clean-shaven. His
features, hair color and the slightly stooped attitude in which he carried himself all contributed to
Austin Loring's looking his age of fifty-six. Only
when he was overtired or sunk into a slough of
depression did he appear to be much older. But in
the two and a half years since the marriage vows
were exchanged, there had been few times when
she had seen him in either state: just once when
without reason he felt cause to doubt her love for
him and now and again when his early plans for
the building of the chapel suffered setbacks. For
the rest, Austin Henry Loring practiced fortitude in
the face of hardship, tolerance toward his fellow
man, and a sometimes irritating faith that the Lord
will help those who help themselves.

"Norah, my dear." Not until her husband spoke
to her was she startled out of a dreamlike, sopo-
rific state of detachment from her surroundings.
And became apprehensively aware that an expec-
tant silence had descended on the part-built chapel
as Austin gazed quizzically at her and the Indians
peered stoically to the north. "My, you were miles
away just then. Do you think we can stretch what's
in the pot to fill four more plates."

He gestured with a hand in the direction the

braves were looking and now Norah gazed behind the wagon and across the curve of sun-glinting railroad track. And her frown of foreboding took a firmer hold on her pale-complexioned face as her squinting eyes focused upon a quartet of horsemen. Seen almost at the limit of vision, they emerged from the shimmering heat haze, closing with the construction site at every slow pace taken by the horses.

Norah felt suddenly and strangely chill in the heat of the day, then discovered she needed to make a conscious effort to drag her anxious eyes away from the distant riders; seeing that Austin, too, showed signs of trepidation. But then he clapped his hands sharply and vented a deep laugh that sounded only slightly less than spontaneous. And probably the livestock and the fire and the stew in the pot had never ceased making sounds—it was just that Norah had been too involved with a strange inner tension to hear what was happening in the real world until Austin's double signal. She was a little less disconcerted by her response to the approach of the riders when she saw that some of the Indians were also discomfited, as her husband chided:

"Come, come! Anyone would think what we are doing here is a guilty secret about to be uncovered! For a moment there, I even found myself affected by your dismay." He laughed again and this time it sounded purely of a joke against himself. "Well, my dear, what of the food? If the strangers accept the invitation I intend to give them, will it stretch? From the delicious aroma, I would guess lunch is almost ready?''

"If each of us has a little less, there'll be enough to go around, Austin," Norah said.

"A little less for somebody and he will not be so round," he answered, mopping the sweat off his grinning face with a forearm as he poked the forefinger of his other hand into the bulbous flesh hanging over the waistband of the Cheyenne's pants.

This brave and some of the other Indians laughed too loudly at the minister's joke. Most, in common with Norah Loring, remained unsettled by the approach of the strangers and had no inclination to try to conceal this as they went to clean up ready for eating. Austin Loring could not fail to be conscious of the apprehension that was heavy in the hot air normally filled with the babble of voices as he shared in the communal washing facilities. And when he and the Indians were clean of dirt from their hands and faces, but not of the sweat of tension instead of exertion, he captured their attention away from the approaching riders by announcing:

"Remember, my friends . . ." He glanced toward Norah. ". . . and my wife. The good Lord takes care of his own."

"There is another saying of the white-eyes, Mr. Loring," one of the Comanches countered in a funereal tone that made him the center of attention. Most gazes sought to focus on the riders again after the brave explained: "It is that the good die young."

Chapter Two

THE four men who reined their mounts to a halt in an uneven line between the rear of the wagon and the railroad track did nothing to dispel the consternation that was so clearly seen on the faces of the ten Indian braves. Norah Loring was able to hide her nervousness behind a fragile smile because one arm of her broadly grinning husband was curled around the back of her waist.

One of the strangers was past forty and the others were all about thirty. The oldest man was broad across the shoulders, barrel-chested and thick-waisted. He was half a head shorter than the others, who were all in the region of six feet tall and built on lean lines. All of them were unshaven and unwashed for many days and their clothes looked and smelled to have been slept in for a number of nights. The man with light-blue eyes and iron-gray hair was handsome despite the grime and bristles on his face. The oldest of the four looked positively ugly while the other two perhaps would be quite good-looking when turned out at their best. One of these was chewing on a soggy wad of tobacco and the other was halfway through smoking a fat cigar.

The eyes of all of them were red-rimmed and each was slumped in an attitude of weariness in his saddle. Each had a revolver in a holster hung from the right side of his gunbelt and a rifle in a forward-slung boot on his saddle. The horses they rode were all chestnut geldings, the animals showing as many signs of travel weariness as the riders.

"Welcome to the site of the Chapel of the Rock of Jesus, friends," Loring greeted expansively, after the quartet had taken perhaps two seconds to make an uncommunicative survey of the white couple standing to one side of the cooking fire, the huddle of Indians on the other side and the part-built chapel. "We would all be most pleased if you will join Mrs. Loring and myself and our Indian brothers for a meal."

"The Chapel of what rock?" the dark-haired, dark-eyed, tobacco chewer asked in a monotone as he spared a disinterested glance for the out-crop, then immediately looked back at the woman with his former expression of arrogant appraisal.

Loring felt his wife quiver in the arc of his arm and took a firmer grip around her waist, trying to hide his own nervousness as he raked his gaze back and forth along the line of four un-smiling faces. He sounded and looked pathetically obsequious when he explained: "It is not the right time of the day. Much better during the second hour after sunup. And it is best viewed from the southeast, friends. But if you will look up toward the top of the rock, not right to the top . . ." He gestured with his free hand and the cigar smoker, the handsome man and the oldest one all looked with no sign of interest in the direction he indicated. ". . . I think you will be able to see more than a mere suggestion of the facial features of a man as they have been shaped on the rock by the elements. Seen at the ideal time, my friends, the face is plainly that of the Lord Jesus Christ, and it is my belief that I was chosen—"

Norah trembled again, and a muffled sound of fear escaped her throat. Her husband dragged his gaze away from the high rock face and saw that the tobacco-chewing man was working his jaw at a frenetic pace, and spilling juice down his bristled, dirt-grimed chin as he moved a hand rhythmically at his crotch.

"I don't see no face, Red, do you?" the man with iron-gray hair asked dully.

"Sure don't, Frank," the oldest and ugliest of the four answered in the same tone. Then he sniffed noisily and showed crooked teeth in a grin of relish as he added: "But I sure smell somethin.' Only trouble is, I don't eat . . ."

"Aw shit, Ben," the man smoking the cigar growled with a sneer of contempt as Red's voice trailed away. "Can't you wait until after we've eaten, frig it?"

Ben abruptly froze into immobility—except for his coal-black eyes that lost their glitter of lust and became dull with self-reproach as he shifted his gaze from the tremulous Norah Loring to peer at his partners.

"Gee, Red, it's been so long I didn't even know I was doin' it," Ben excused, snatched his hand away from himself and spat out the wad of tobacco.

". . . I don't fancy eatin' my food with the stink of Injuns up my nose," Red went on, as if there had been no interruption. But then, against an apprehensive gabble and an anxious stirring of movement among the Indians, he revealed he was aware of what the sexually aroused man had been doing. "And Barr's right, Ben, you horny sonofabitch. The dessert comes last. And it ain't a matter of help yourself today." The grin returned to his heavy-featured face as his small, green eyes became fixed on the pulsating-with-fear bosom of Norah Loring. "Not when we got us such a pretty little lady to serve us with whatever we find appealin'."

Now all four men were grinning lasciviously as for stretched seconds they fastened their bright-eyed gazes on the woman, who suddenly felt terror turn the sweat ice-cold on her flesh as their gazes seemed with palpable force to penetrate her gown, then shifted to convey approval to her petrified face of what they had seen.

"Gentlemen, I beg of you . . ." her husband started to plead, his voice thick with stupefying shock, as Norah tore her eyes free of the strangers' leering faces and swung her head to look at the twitching cheek of the man at her side. And now she extended an arm around his narrow waist, but to clasp him in the manner of one giving rather than seeking reassurance. His prominent Adam's apple bobbed and he hurried on: "Take our food, our wagon, our animals—everything we possess that you covet. But please do not harm my wife or our fellow toilers who are here to do God's will."

The braves had curtailed their fearful whisperings and apprehensive stirrings while the preacher made his entreaty. But as soon as he was through, the noise and movement began once more. And there was suddenly panic in the hot, sunlit air that caused Norah Loring to wrench her head around again. Her intention was to look away from the death-mask profile of Austin, ignore the lecherous strangers, and attempt by word, expression or deed to offer some brand of comfort to the Indians. But then she saw what had triggered her husband's dread and erupted terror in the minds of the braves.

"Oh, no!" she tried to shriek, but the appeal emerged from her constricted throat as a hoarse whisper. While, for a stretched second, she was utterly immobile; rooted to the spot and locked against the side of Austin as if by some invisible claw. This as the ugly Red slid the rifle from the boot on his saddle and the three younger men raked their gazes away from her to look at him and then imitate his move.

"One thing I just can't abide is the stink of Injuns," Red growled. "And I reckon that if I was to try to eat the food you've so kindly offered me and the boys, reverend . . . well, there's a good chance their stink would cause me to sick it right up again.''

Some of the braves whirled and lunged across the campsite, a few intent upon reaching the cluster of wickiups and laying their hands on guns and the more traditional Indian weapons; while others angled toward the cover of the unfinished chapel and nearby heaps of building supplies. One stood in abject terror and two more powered forward, hysterical hatred supplanting their earlier panic as they reached out with bare, clawed hands. Austin Henry Loring snatched his arm from around the waist of his wife and turned to face the outcrop in back of the chapel in the making, before he dropped to his knees and clasped his hands in front of his chest, his lips working to silently mouth the words of a prayer. This as his wife, turned from the waist, brought up both hands to press the palms tight to her ears while her eyes darted back and forth along the shock-widened sockets. And the Henry repeater of Red and the Spencers of the other three horsemen exploded shot after shot into the flesh of the helpless Apaches, Comanches and the lone Cheyenne.

The white men laughed in sadistic enjoyment of the merciless killing. The raucous sounds venting from their gaping mouths rang louder in the blocked ears of the woman than did the crack of bullets from the rifle muzzles. The puffs of smoke that accompanied the firing of each shot looked

15

very white to her. The blood that gushed from wounds was vividly crimson. The smell of the gunsmoke was so pungent she thought she might vomit when she sucked it down her throat.

Abruptly, all the braves fell on the rough, arid, much-trampled ground, most of them sprawled in attitudes of utter immobility that told unequivocally of their death. While, here and there in the sudden silence that existed under the pressing palms of Norah Loring, her never-still eyes saw an arm twitch, a leg jerk, a head roll or an entire body spasm. She gaped her mouth wide then, to vent a scream that was so loud within her own mind she failed to hear the fusillade of revolver shots. But, try as she might, she was unable to force herself to close her eyes or avert them from the scene of the continuing carnage. Thus she saw more blood-gouting wounds blasted into vulnerable flesh—and witnessed the final dust-raising movements of the dead braves as their nervous systems enacted a final response.

She moved her hands from her ears to her throat to augment the effort of will to keep the fluid nausea out of her throat. And as she did so she heard the final growls of laughter trickle from the throats of the callous killers as they sat astride their unconcerned mounts, while the team horses and Indian ponies in the remuda began to calm after being spooked by the gunfire.

"Well, that's fine, just fine," Red announced with a sigh." Again he set the pattern for the others by ejecting the spent cartridge cases from his Remington six-shooter and pushing fresh rounds into the empty chambers. "About ready to eat now. Ain't nothin' like completin' a worthwhile chore for sharpenin' a man's appetite, is my opinion."

"Hey, preacherman!" the man named Barr said irritably, and struck a match on the butt of his revolver as he slid it into the holster. He relit his cigar which had gone out while he was taking part in the slaughter of the Indians. "I don't reckon you need say no grace on account of us boys. We ain't of a religious disposition."

They all laughed again, as they swung down from their saddles and the reins of all the mounts were given to Ben, who moved to hitch them to the tailgate of the wagon. But, although he was still down on his knees, Loring was no longer praying: as the rifles were booted and the revolvers were drawn he had allowed his hands to drop limply to the ground at his sides while he stared in grimacing horror at the concluding acts of the slaughter.

"Norah, my dear, I'm so sorry," he said in a hushed whisper as Red, Barr and Frank advanced on them. "I and my God have failed you."

"No, Austin," the woman countered in a dull tone that matched the look in her gray eyes that had begun to spill silent tears. "He is not just your God, my good and fine husband. He is *our* God. And if this be His will, I do not question it."

The danger of her being sick to her stomach was gone, and she was able to release the strangle-like hold on her own throat and extend a hand toward the kneeling man. But he felt a compelling need to get to his feet unaided. Struggling to come unsteadily erect, he stared fixedly at the scattering of bullet-riddled corpses and attempted to find hatred for the killers while he tried to make himself deaf to what they were saying.

"Vegetable slop is all, Red," Barr said grouchily after stirring the contents of the cooking pot, then took up a ladleful and scowled his distaste as he emptied it back again.

"Thought I didn't smell no meat," the good-looking Frank complained.

"I got some meat," Ben put in as he joined the others at the fire, but ignored the bubbling stew to look salaciously at the woman. "But it ain't to be shared with you guys. It's the kind that's only for feedin' to pussies."

He vented a shrill laugh and once more both his hands went to his crotch; his eyes glittering while he seemed to be unaware of what he was doing to himself.

"You keep on like that, buddy," Red said contemptuously, "and you'll squeeze all the juice outta the meat before—"

"Frig it!" Ben snarled in self-anger, and wrenched his hands away as if they had suddenly been burned.

"Course, it's all a matter of personal preference," Red said, now as disinterested in the food as the younger men. "But me, I'd rather have the pretty little lady chew the fat."

Frank and Barr vented giggling laughter in response to this. But both Red and Ben were too absorbed in the vivid imagery of sexual anticipation to be sidetracked. This as the skinny, frail-looking, gaunt-faced Loring at last experienced the fires of malevolence burning deep inside of him. But he knew, at the same time—as Norah took a firm hold on his upper arm and kept him from stumbling—the bitter shame of being helpless to strike a blow against the loathsome enemy.

"Guess you wanna be first, Red?" Ben asked huskily.

"No, Ben," the older, uglier, more heavy-set, less outwardly aroused man answered. "I doubt you'd be able to wait for me. You go ahead and enjoy her. Don't reckon I'll have to wait long."

Ben expelled a whistling breath and stepped around the fire, a strange expression of almost childish joy on his filthy and bristled face. And, in keeping with this look, there was a kind of over-excited self-consciousness in his tone when he said: "I don't know about you, girl, but I ain't so keen to be bare ass ballin' out in the open. In the back of the wagon, okay?"

"You will not put a finger on my wife, you murdering, lusting brutes!" Loring thundered. And made to take a forward step.

"No, Austin," Norah said, her tone icy-calm and her grip on his arm suddenly much more firm. And when he checked the move and swung his head to look at her, he found it almost unreal that the expression on her beautiful, pale, tear-stained face was a match for the cold serenity which had sounded in her voice. "Please don't allow them to blemish your blameless life. If such a man as you is not able to obey His Commandments in the face of provocation—''

''Frig that, God talk spooks me!'' Ben snarled. And he closed with Norah as she let go her hold on her husband and stepped between the two men. ''Keep an eye on the preacher, you guys.''

He brought his right arm up and reached forward, dirt-grimed hand clawed to delve into the reddish-blonde hair and fasten a grip on the nape of her neck. For a moment, Norah seemed poised to resist him, remained rigid with her feet planted rock-steady on the ground as she shot a backward glance at her husband. And, through the tears of helplessness that clouded his vision, it seemed to Austin Loring that she showed him a fleeting smile. She swung her head to face the lusting younger man and allowed herself to be lurched submissively against him.

Ben vented another whistling breath, Barr emitted a shrill yell of encouragement, Frank spoke a low-toned obscenity and Red sent a globule of saliva into the flames beneath the cooking pot.

''Dear God and sweet Lord Jesus in Heaven!'' Loring pleaded, and turned from the waist, thrusting his clawed hands high into the air like he was trying to reach out and touch the area of limestone eroded into the shape of a human face.

''It's His will, my darling husband!'' Norah shrieked. And twisted free of Ben's grip just as he was about to encircle her with his free arm. ''You

must not break the Commandments and neither
will I!''

''Shit!'' Frank screamed.

''Goddamit!'' Red bellowed.

''Red, she's got my gun!''

''Stupid bastard!'' Barr growled with enough
vehemence to force the cigar free of his teeth and
send it into the cooking pot.

Ben had instinctively thrust his arms into the air
as he shrieked what everybody but Austin Loring
had seen for himself. And part of a second later
the men on the far side of the fire all reached for
their holstered revolvers. Then, as the preacher
again abandoned an entreaty to the impassive rock
face to rake his tear-blurred eyes to the scene at
ground level, Ben let his arms flop to his sides and
the other three stayed their hands on the gun butts.
And all five men stared in varying degrees of
horror at the woman who became as composed as
she had been moments before and spoke in the
same even tone to say:

''We shalt not kill, my dear Austin.''

She closed her lips around the barrel of the Remington, pushed back the hammer with the thumb of
her left hand and squeezed the trigger with the
forefinger of her right. The sound of the gunshot
was muffled within the soft flesh of Norah Loring's
mouth. She died instantly on her feet and toppled
in a rigid attitude, the big hat falling off her head
to show the ugly stain of blood in her hair from the
exit wound. Just a little run of blood spilled from
the side of her mouth as she slammed against the

hard ground, her legs straight and demurely together while her arms were flung out to the sides,
the gun with the slickly smeared muzzle hurled
clear of her open hand.

"Careless bastard!" Frank paraphrased Barr's
response.

"What a friggin' waste of a good-lookin' piece
of tail," Barr muttered.

"Goddammit, nobody else spotted she might do
somethin' like that!" Ben excused.

"That's right, buddy," Red allowed, moving
his again weary-eyed gaze from the corpse of Norah
Loring to where her husband stood, looking on the
point of passing out—or maybe even dying. But
then, as if by some magical transfer of inner strength
from the dead body into the living one, Austin
Henry Loring no longer looked drained and frail
and much older than his years. Neither was he
afraid of nor any more filled with hatred for the
men he now surveyed with much the same brand
of equanimity as his wife had shown during the
final few seconds of her life. He came rigidly erect
after curtailing the initial impulse to drop to his
knees beside the corpse of Norah, and there was a
glint of something akin to contemptuous pride in
his sunken eyes as he gazed through the distorting
smoke-and-heat shimmer above the fire and invited evenly:

"You may do it whenever you are ready."

"What?" Red asked, frowning his bewilderment.

"And in whatever manner pleases you."

22

"I think he's gone outta his head, Red," Frank growled, and seemed afraid to be near a lunatic.

"He sure as hell is crazy, you guys!" Ben snarled as he snatched up the blood-smeared gun thrown from Norah's dead hand. "What the nutty preacher is sayin' is that he's ready to get his! And we can do it any which way that we like. Which is mighty big of him considerin' he ain't in no state to—"

"Yeah, Ben, I got his drift now," Red cut in as the younger man cleaned the blood and dust off his gun under his armpit.

"Red, I'm through here," the blue-eyed, prematurely gray-haired Frank said, attempting to mask his nervousness with a forced attitude of boredom. "Let's just blast the sonofabitch and get the hell out of here."

"I'm for that," Ben agreed eagerly, and checked his move to push the Remington into his holster.

"I ain't so sure about killin' a man of the cloth," Barr argued, as he lit a fresh cigar with a flaming piece of fire kindling.

The imperturbably unresisting Austin Henry Loring looked openly into the face of each man who spoke and his gaunt features did not alter their opinion. Then, like the three younger men, he directed his unblinking gaze toward the leader by common consent; and waited with more patience than they did for Red to reach a decision on his fate, in a silence kept from being absolute by the crackle of the fire, the bubbling of the stew, the subdued sounds made by the livestock and the rising and falling hum of swarms of flies voraciously gorging on the rapidly drying blood of eleven corpses.

"You ain't gonna put up no fight, yellowbelly preacherman?" Red rasped scornfully, at length.

"If I needed to be reminded of my lifelong-held belief—"

"Yeah, yeah, yeah," Red cut in with sour intolerance. "Not only not killin' and stealin' and all them other Sunday church laws, preacherman. I heard what she said before she ate the lead. Guess you go in for that turnin' the other cheek crap, too?"

"Red, we didn't oughta pull his pecker about what he believes in," Barr warned, and backed off toward where his horse was hitched at the rear of the wagon—looking anxiously about himself as if he suspected some mysterious power was lurking nearby, poised to attack him.

"Frig it, I'm with Frank," Red snapped. "With the tail dead and one of Barr's soggy-with-spit cigars messin' up the grub in the pot, there ain't nothin' to keep us here. Ben, go bring your lariat."

Ben went to do Red's bidding, his coal-black eyes bright with excited anticipation of what was to come. He took a piece of fresh chewing tobacco out of his saddlebag and was noisily masticating juice from it as he extended the coil of rope toward Red.

"We gonna string him up, drag him or what?"

The bigger-framed man shook his head and moved around the fire with a gesture that the eager younger man should follow him. In his own small, green eyes there was an expression of contempt and triumph not dissimilar to that which the preacher had displayed earlier.

"Turn around," he instructed as he halted three feet in front of Loring, both men standing beside the corpse of Norah. "I wanna see if you got a streak down your back to match your yellowbelly."

"Red, I ain't religious, you know that, but I don't go for—"

"I ain't gonna kill him, Barr," Red cut in on the complaint. Then he sighed through a grin as the preacher obeyed the instruction—drew the Remington from his holster and tossed it a few inches into the air: just enough so that he could fist his hand around the barrel of the revolver. Next he pushed it higher and out to the side, and whipped it back along a short arc, to crash the base of the butt into the side of Loring's head between his right ear and the underside of his hat brim.

If the preacher experienced a bolt of pain from the point of the impact, he had no time to vent a cry: he was unconscious on his feet and so certainly felt nothing as he corkscrewed downward and sprawled on his side at right angles to Norah's corpse. The blow had not broken the skin beneath the matting of gray hair so there was no blood on the man's head.

"He's still breathin' his God's pure air," Red growled as he cast a sneering glance at where Frank and Barr stood holding the unhitched reins of their horses. Then he guffawed and added: "So

I figure I ain't muffed my chance of gettin' through them Pearly Gates!''

Then, the laughter reduced to a grin of evil intent, he holstered the gun and with the eager help of the giggling Ben put into effect the scheme that had occurred to his warped mind while he nurtured his anger toward the unresponsive preacher. He drew a knife from a sheath at the back of his belt but, to the sighing relief of Barr and the impatient scowl of Frank, used the sharply honed blade only to cut the lariat into short lengths and to slice through the fabric of the Lorings' clothing. And, less than ten minutes after the gun butt crashed into the preacher's head, Red and Ben were finished: and the three younger men followed the example of their older mentor in swinging up astride the horses. They spent just a second or so looking down with either grins or grimaces at the result of Red's and Ben's handiwork.

Both the dead woman and the senseless man had been stripped naked—the clothing cut from their bodies scattered carelessly over the campsite. Then Norah had been arranged on her back with her legs splayed and Austin was placed face down on top of her. His ankles were tied together and so were those of the woman, but interlocked at the small of Austin's back. His forearms were bound beneath her head and her wrists were tied at a midway point between his shoulder blades. To complete the gruesome and obscene tableau, a length of timber staking had been driven into the ground at either side of Norah's head. They projected high enough to reach above the man's head, and hold it firmly in the position that placed his lips hard against her blood-filled mouth.

"You get some twisted notions every now and then, Red," Frank growled as he tugged on the reins and heeled his mount into movement.

"Appealed to me as a real fittin' climax," the grinning Red countered.

"Climax!" Ben yelled, and then laughed so forcefully his wad of tobacco was ejected. "Shit, that's a good one, old buddy!"

He moved his horse in the wake of Frank's mount.

"I ain't so sure I wouldn't have preferred to see you put a bullet in him," Barr muttered morosely. "That's gonna be a bad way to die."

He had taken the dead cigar from between his teeth to speak. Now he hung it back there but did not relight it as he clucked his mount into a slow walk behind the other two.

"Nah, it's real fittin' just like I said," Red argued as he cast a final, self-satisfied look over the area surrounding the unfinished chapel. "There he is—a preacherman out front of his church, with his flock of one-time heathen Injuns that he must've converted, set to die in the arms of his everlovin' wife."

He spurred his horse into a faster start than the others, intent upon catching up with them. "And what's more, yellowbelly!" he taunted a man who could not hear him, "you're gonna die in what I hear is called the missionary position.''

His raucous burst of laughter once again disturbed the team horses and Indian ponies in the remuda.

Chapter Three

THE man who sat in the rocker on the stoop of the Aurora Restaurant in midtown Prospect gave the impression of being at peace with himself and with the world about him. And there was no indication as he relished the cigarette he smoked and the coffee he sipped, that he missed anything of note on the main street of this small Texas town. He appeared not to look at anything in particular.

This early spring evening, with the weather warm and the sky clear and star-spangled and half-moon lit, he was what he appeared to be as he took his ease and quietly enjoyed a sense of well-being, though he remained to a degree alert to the possibility that this state of affairs might come to an end. For life had conditioned this man whose name was Edge not to take anything for granted; certainly not to be lulled into a false sense of security after a time of good and easy living during which trouble of any kind had not even brushed the outer limits of his tranquil existence.

The life that had taught this man the hard way that he had to take his ease whenever opportunity presented but always to be prepared for a violent shattering of his peace, was more than forty years long. And even when he was in repose, his face revealed to the perceptive observer that many of the years had been crowded with harsh experiences. Even clearer to be seen in the time-lined and element-burnished face of Edge was the fact that he was of mixed parentage. The mixture was northern European and Hispanic—his mother had been an immigrant from Scandinavia and his father was a Mexican. The survivor of the dead parents' two sons was a man who could be considered either handsome or totally devoid of good looks: the opinions divided by responses to the suggestion of latent cruelty discernible in his eyes and the set of his mouthline. Some, maybe the most perceptively discerning of people in his past, had claimed that there was much more than just a mere suggestion of the evil that lurked within the man: that his capacity to unleash brutality on those who crossed him was blatantly obvious—even when he was as placidly composed as he was on this pleasant evening in Prospect, Texas.

His eyes were ice-blue and had a cold glitter in even the faintest of lights. Their lids were permanently narrowed, like he was always in the brightest of lights. The upper ones were hooded. His mouth was broad and thin-lipped, with above and to the sides an unobtrusive Mexican-style moustache, while his jawline was firm and suggestive of aggression. His cheekbones were high and prominent and between was a nose that was aquiline in shape. His hair was thick and worn long enough to reach below his shirt collar. The same shade of grayness that could be seen amid the jet-black hair showed up more obviously in his bristles when he needed to shave.

It was a hard, lean face. And his frame was hard and lean, too—he was six feet three inches tall and weighed a proportionately packed two hundred pounds.

He was dressed all in black: riding boots without spurs worn inside the cuffs of his pants, a gunbelt with a Frontier Colt in the holster which was not at the moment held by the toe ties down to his right thigh, shirt, kerchief and Stetson, all of this relatively new except for the revolver. And what he wore beneath the topclothes was recently store-bought with a single exception—the circle of dull-colored beads on a thong around his neck under the kerchief with, hung at the nape under his shirt, a leather pouch that contained an open straight razor.

Throughout the entire winter just past, while he spent some time in Arizona, old and New Mexico and latterly Texas, he had needed to draw the razor only to shave. He had not once fired the .45 revolver, nor the Winchester rifle that was with the rest of his gear in his room at Mrs. Doyle's boardinghouse down at the southern end of the main street, since he rode away from what was left of what must have been the strangest and most ill-fated whorehouse on the frontier.

He had drifted through bigger and smaller, dirtier and cleaner, livelier and duller, better and worse towns than Prospect as he rode whatever trail took his fancy whenever he took it into his head to move on, purchasing whatever he or his chestnut gelding needed and just occasionally indulging in what he felt he wanted—from the stake that was just a little less than four thousand dollars at the start of winter. Just the new clothes from a store in Santa Fe, a new saddle and accoutrements from a leathersmith at El Paso, a replacement bedroll with cooking and eating utensils bought from a down-on-his-luck drifter at a rockbottom price outside of Arizpe in Sonora, infrequent nights of bed and board in hotels or rooming houses and even rarer meals in restaurants like the Aurora, had cost him money over and above that spent on the necessities. And, all in all, this had not been an excessive drain on his resources, and that he still had close to two thousand dollars between himself and poverty contributed just as much to his seemingly lethargic feeling of contentment as did the warm glow from having a full belly and the anticipation of sleeping under a roof between crisp, clean bedsheets.

Did he want a drink before he made tracks down the broad, quiet, sparsely lit street to Mrs. Doyle's boardinghouse? He pondered this idly as he continued to sip the strong, black coffee and watched the progess of a buggy and two-horse team as the rig came slowly toward the midtown area from the north. A drink of beer or liquor, he corrected himself as he arced the cigarette butt out of the moon shadow and over the rail of the stoop to the dusty, wheel-rutted and hoof-printed street. He did not have to wonder whether he had differentiated between *want* and *need*. He was never confused between these two quite separate demands that were made upon a man from within.

Diagonally up and across the main street from the single-story, frame-built Aurora Restaurant which was on the east side, was the two-story, brick and timber Best in the West saloon. When the restaurant closed up for the night—and the coffee-drinking half-breed was the last patron on the premises— the Best in the West would be one of just two commercial enterprises in Prospect still lit and open. The other was the railroad depot that was at the northern end of the street, but this was dimly lit and occupied by only two disgruntled railroadmen awaiting the arrival of an overdue freight train. The entire lower floor of the saloon was brightly lit, the yellow light of several kerosene lamps spilling out through the frosted-glass windows and the batwinged doorway across the roofed sidewalk. Also, two of the five upper-floor windows allowed a little light to escape through the cracks where drapes failed to meet at the center, these narrow fingers of illumination falling onto the railed balcony of the sidewalk roof. And there sounded to be many more than just two people in the place—the talk and laughter of the patrons and staff competing with the clink of glass on glass, the chink of money changing hands, the rattle of the machinery of some games of chance and the off-key clanging and thudding of a dilapidated player piano. In total, this noise that seemed to float out of the saloon on drifting tobacco smoke was not overly obtrusive, though, even in such a quiet country town as Prospect.

The door behind and to the left of Edge opened and the round-faced and round-bodied man who did the cooking at the Aurora asked diffidently: "Pardon me, sir, but I reckon you wouldn't have no objection if me and the wife closed up the place now? You just leave your empty cup on the stoop there when you've finished."

Edge drained the cup down to the dregs and held it out toward the nervous man. "I'm through and I've no objection, feller. The supper was the best I've eaten in a long time."

The fat man beamed his appreciation of the compliment as his wife who waited at table began to douse the lamps in the small and clean restaurant behind him. "Real nice of you to say so, sir. All our meat and game is fresh from the ranches and the country nearby. And the vegetables are local grown, from the farms around town and some in our own yard out back. Oh, dear, I can't say I like the look of that."

The husband and wife who ran the restaurant had not liked the look of the half-breed when he rode into Prospect from the south this afternoon: unshaven, sweat-run and with his flesh and cloth-

ing powdered by trail dust, weary from the heat
and the long miles of travel, so in no humor to
alter the natural impassive set of his face to even
hint at a smile, and thus looking grudgeful, mean
and maybe ready to use the handgun in his holster
or the rifle in the boot against whoever unwittingly
riled him over the line in back of which his dark
anger was under control. Edge had sensed the
homesteaders in the fields and front yards of the
places which flanked the south trail eyeing him
with surreptitious apprehension as he rode toward
the town. He experienced at close quarters the
uneasiness he had triggered in the local citizenry
when he led his mount into the livery stable of Joel
Slocum and again from the women and old men on
the street as he moved among them on foot, heading with his heavy load of gear toward the boardinghouse of Mrs. Doyle that the liveryman had
recommended as the best place in town for a
passing-through stranger to rest up. And Mrs. Cloris
Doyle was more than a little perturbed by her first
impression of the man who tracked dust and brought
a bad smell into her scrupulously clean and fresh-
aired place.

It was nothing new in the experience of the
half-breed for his first appearance in a quiet community to provoke such nervousness and suspicion
among peaceable people. For it was a long time
since he had slotted neatly into the pattern of
conformity that was essential if a man was to be
comfortably accepted as one of the crowd against
the conventional backdrop. During this same length

of time, he had always elected to go his own way in his own manner and leave those around him to keep their initial impression of him or change their views according to his actions, unless somebody ventured to question him, when he would volunteer some placatory information about himself and his reasons for being where he was—sometimes.

This afternoon and evening in the town of Prospect, nobody asked him any personal questions, not even the local lawman whose office Edge passed on his stroll from the boardinghouse to the restaurant and who looked out through the half-curtained window with something stronger than idle curiosity in his eyes. But by this time the stranger was washed up and shaved and had dusted off this clothes, looked a little rested up and cooled down and not so apparently ready to go for his gun at the least provocation. He still looked a trifle too capable of taking care of himself without a thought for the welfare of others, maybe; he still did not offer the first word of greeting to other strollers, nor invite others to greet him; and spruced up better than most of the local citizens he still quite obviously was not and never could be as one with them. But those who had not witnessed his arrival in Prospect were pleasantly surprised that he was not the brutish ogre they had imagined him to be from the gossip that had been spread about him. While those who had instigated the tall stories were now inclined to believe what Joel Slocum and Cloris Doyle had said about the stranger's unlikely good manners in his dealings with them.

"Not trouble, Avery?" the wife of the cook asked anxiously as she moved onto the threshold behind him and peered out over his shoulder.

The man who climbed stiffly down from the buggy which he had rolled to a halt out front of the Best in the West, stretched his aching limbs, flexed his set muscles and kneaded his weary eyes with his fists, did not to any degree look like he was bringing to Prospect the kind of trouble which Edge was suspected of harboring. But the woman, who had automatically glanced at the half-breed sitting easily in the rocker to seek the cause of her husband's concern, showed a frown that was a match for the one on his fleshy face after she shifted her gaze toward the second stranger to come to town today.

"Golly, a preacher," she muttered.

He seemed to be an old man, the best part of six feet tall with a stoop-shouldered frame that came close to being emaciated—he probably did not weigh as much as a hundred and thirty pounds. His face was as angular as his body had to be beneath the black frock coat, black shirt with grubby white cleric's collar and pants with the cuffs pushed into boots laced with string—every item of his garb at least two sizes too large for him. He was seen to be almost totally bald before he reached into the buggy to bring out and don a gray Stetson with a black band that was as old and ill-used as the rest of his clothing, but fitted him better. While his face was as yet unshadowed by the broad brim of the hat, it could be seen that he had deep-set eyes of a light color beneath prominent brows. His sharp nose was also prominent and he had a slack, perhaps toothless, mouth above a jutting chin. He either had an unkempt salt-and-pepper embryo beard or had neglected to shave for several days.

The roofed and backed but sideless four-wheeled buggy he stood beside as he buttoned his coat and surveyed the street with a strange brand of melancholic resentment looked to be as dilapidated as he. And the pair of sway-backed gray geldings in the traces were in no better condition.

"Prospect people have an aversion to parsons?" Edge asked as the newcomer shuffled wearily around the front of his team and stepped up onto the sidewalk like a man with cramp in one leg, then stood in the light from the batwinged entrance of the saloon. For a second or so he seemed reluctant to enter the place, but then he took a black-bound book from a pocket of his frock coat and pulled his hunched shoulders almost erect before he pushed through the doors and strode inside.

"We have us the finest Presbyterian church in northwest Texas and maybe the finest minister of the faith in the whole of the state of preach in it, sir," the fat man countered in a hurt and defensive tone. "Even if as the organist down at the church I'm biased, I don't reckon there's many who know of such things who'd take issue with me on either count."

"Townspeople are God-fearin' and church-goin' for the most part," his wife augmented. "Includin' some of them that work at the Best in the West.

But Frank Crowell ain't that kind, mister. Nice enough man for the owner of such a place, but he has a strange and powerful hate for anythin' and everythin' that smacks of religion.''

She raised her voice to complete what she was saying, to ensure Edge could hear her words above the abrupt increase of sound from the brightly lit building across the street, the clamor comprised mostly of voices raised in the tone of both anger and derision. Then this swell subsided and just a single voice was shouting against the unmelodious music of the discordant player piano and the almost tuneful, by comparison, clicking and whirring of the wheel of fortune, roulette wheel and dice birdcages, the voice of a man, his words indistinct to the listeners on the stoop of the restaurant until the mechanical devices with which he was competing were one by one silenced.

''. . . and I say to you, friends, my brothers and my sisters, that there is still time to repent and to be granted the forgiveness of the Lord Jesus Christ! To pave the way to living in one of the many mansions of His and our father, Almighty God! Time to abandon the whoring and the wagering on games of chance! The lewd and lecherous ways encouraged by strong drink for which such dens of iniquity as this were created by the disciples of Satan! I surely ask little enough of you here and now? Just a few meager seconds of your time and your attention! So that I may read a text from the Good Book—that you may think upon it at a quieter period! And perhaps feel moved to attend your local church here in Prospect! The spire of which served to give me a bearing by which I was able to steer a course for—''

"Preacher!" another man thundered, and the single word, vented like it was an obscenity, dripped with ominous menace.

"That's Frank," Avery whispered.

"Oh, golly," his wife murmured.

"My brother, come down and join us in a reading—''

"Turn around and get your ass outta my place, preacher," Frank Crowell cut in, speaking not so loudly now. But strangely there seemed to be more force behind the words: the mere sound of them painting an image of the dark scowl of depthless, enraged hatred that surely had to be on the face of the saloon owner. "Because if you don't do that, I'll do it for you. With the toe of my shoe up your asshole so hard you'll hit the center of the street on your head."

"Friend, brother . . . there can be redemption even for such a disciple of Satan as you who is the—''

"Start the pianola, dammit. Get those wheels turnin' and the cards dealt. There's a drink on the house for everyone here. And I ain't talkin' brews. Best sippin' whiskey for you guys. Champagne for the girls. And I'll waive the house cut on every tumble that's taken tonight. Celebrate the first preacher's ass I've gotten to kick since I don't recall when. Go to it!"

There was utter silence while Crowell made the

announcement. But mounting excitement could be sensed in the saloon as his tone got louder and the angry menace gave way to exuberance—which was matched and quickly surpassed by the tumult of cheering and handclapping and laughing and yelling that exploded in response to his generosity.

"Oh, dear," Avery said.

"Good night, sir," his wife said, then hurried to add: "I hope if you remain in town for any length of time you will patronize the Aurora again. Come, Avery."

"Yes, Ruth."

They backed off the threshold and closed the door of the darkened restaurant; turned a key and shot a bolt at the top and the bottom. But Edge did not hear their footfalls retreating among the white-covered, chair-ringed tables and guessed they were watching through the net-curtained window on the other side of the doorway as the preacher backed out between the batwings of the Best in the West. The tall, thin old man emerged with much the same brand of reluctance as he had entered only a few seconds earlier. But it was doubtless fear rather than an effort of will that held him rigidly erect. Then, as a much younger man showed on the threshold of the saloon, hands hooked over the tops of the batwings to stop their flapping, the preacher fell.

His gaze seemed to be locked with that of the tall, lean, handsome Crowell while whatever emotion held him in a powerful grip apparently detached him from everything else. For he failed to realize he had backed across the width of the sidewalk, until he sought to lower a booted foot behind him onto solid support. But his foot went down lower than he expected and he was unbalanced before he located the street surface just a few inches beneath the lip of the sidewalk. And he fell back against the flank of one of his horses with a shrill cry of alarm. The blow and the howl spooked the horse, which snorted and lunged forward. And the second gelding responded in like manner to the panic of the first: the two of them able to drag the buggy with the brake-locked wheels behind them.

After the dust of the pumping hooves and the slithering wheelrims had settled, none of the witnesses would have been surprised to see the old man badly injured. But the preacher had not been trampled by flying hooves nor run over by the locked wheels. He was able to rise unsteadily to his feet, still clutching his Bible in both trembling hands. It was not possible for him to appear any thinner, but he certainly looked shorter as he stood on the street, staring fixedly again—but needing to tilt his head and peer up—at the man with iron-gray hair who made no move to push out through the batwing doors.

There was not just Edge and Frank Crowell, Avery and Ruth to watch what was happening now. For the preacher's cry and the sounds of the buggy's frantic lurch into motion had drawn the curious to windows and some doorways along both sides of the midtown stretch of Prospect's main street. Now, more than a hundred yards clear of the area where the panic was caused, and almost winded by the effort of dragging the dead weight of the buggy after a long and hot day out on the trail, the geldings had come to a breathless, head-hanging halt. And there was just the body of sound from behind Crowell to disturb the peace of the town again, and provide a counterpoint of geniality to his embittered enmity as he warned:

"Best you don't just stay clear of my place, preacher! Best you get back aboard that rattletrap and haul your ass right outta this town! On account of the next time I get this close to you, I'll maybe be able to ignore the stink of you and forget what a broken-down old sonofabitch you are! And if I do that, preacher, it won't be the toe of my shoe you'll get up your asshole! Get my drift?"

Now it did seem as if he was about to step outside of the saloon—sideways. But he did not do this: he merely swung into a half turn and pushed open the batwings wide enough to display the gleaming revolver in the high-gloss, cutaway leather holster on his right hip. Then he showed a white-toothed grin that was perhaps even colder than the coldest of which Edge was capable; before he released his grip on the tops of the doors and swung all the way around to move away from the threshold—raucously yelling that it sounded to him like his customers were not really enjoying themselves. This provoked a higher volume of noise, which the preacher turned his back on to walk disconsolately and perhaps painfully down the street in the wake of his buggy and runaway team. His expression hidden in the shadow of his hat brim, the bright glow of the half-moon kept off his skeletal features after he was beyond the reach of the light from the saloon. Nobody watched him from the Best in the West anymore. Edge heard Avery and Ruth withdraw to their living quarters at the rear of the restaurant, and sensed that most other Prospect citizens who had been attracted to witness potential violence were now back at whatever had occupied them previously.

The half-breed dug the makings from a pocket of his shirt and took his time in rolling a cigarette, the decision made: the soft bed and clean sheets in the quietness of his room at the boarding house was more appealing than a drink—even the best sipping whiskey—in the saloon that sounded like it was no different from a hundred others he had spent time in.

He was still tipping tobacco from his poke into the paper when the batwings across the street flapped and he looked up in time to see Frank Crowell emerge from the Best in the West. He had donned a light-gray jacket to match his pants and vest, and also a cream-colored Stetson with an ornate tooled-leather band. The half-breed noticed that the handsome man's black shoes gleamed almost as brightly as his silver-plated, ivory-handled .44 Remington Frontier revolver—the cutaway holster was slung low enough so that the side of the jacket did not drape the gun.

The man stood for a second or so, peering into

infinity with an expression that suggested he was not relishing what he saw there. Then he turned and moved along the sidewalk, his heels rapping hollowly on the boarding. He was out from under the roofed section of the sidewalk along the front of his saloon and starting to pass the façade of the single-story stage line depot next door when one of the unlit upstairs windows of his place was noisily opened. And a woman demanded in a whining, slightly slurred voice:

"That you, Frankie?"

Crowell halted and turned from the waist to look up at where a good-looking, no-longer-young, blonde-haired woman thrust her head and thinly nightgowned shoulders out of the window. "Sure, Marsha. Just gonna take a walk. Breathe some fresh air and get rid of the stink of that preacher from my nostrils."

"You hurry back, you hear, honey."

"You bet. And you better not be so overdressed when I get back, uh?"

She laughed throatily before she closed the window, probably too drunk to discern that the lightness in Crowell's tone had a forced quality. Then the dudishly dressed man continued on his southward course along the west side of the street. While on the stoop of the Aurora Restaurant, Edge completed his unhurried making of the cigarette, lit it with a match struck on the butt of his holstered Colt and then rose out of the rocker. He blew out some smoke on the second half of a part yawn and stepped down from the stoop, to start along the street in the same direction as the old preacher and Crowell.

By then the men were no longer in sight and all that he could see moving on the brightly moonlit and deeply moonshadowed stretch of street were the weary horses, the animals beginning to become restive at being left in the traces for so long where they had halted after their bolt. The buggy was stalled out front of a dry-goods store, across the street from the law office. Like most of the other buildings that flanked the street south of the saloon— and along the streets that ran off to the east and to the west—these two showed no lights. Even rooms in private houses, and in Mrs. Doyle's boarding-house, which were lit by lamp or candle, had the drapes tightly drawn at their windows so that little illumination was wasted through cracks into the night. And it was as peacefully quiet as it was dark on this south side of town, the half-breed's slow-moving footfalls providing the only sounds in the surrounding silence: until he crossed the mouth of a narrow alley between a candy store and a barbering parlor opposite the Prospect Grade School, when a voice pleaded in the inky blackness, some twenty or thirty feet from where Edge came to a halt:

"But, please, I cannot—"

"Shut your mouth, you crazy old sonofabitch!"

The half-breed recognised Frank Crowell as the second man to speak, only then realised the other man in the darkness was the preacher, his voice sounding entirely different when it was not raised to sermonize.

"But there is nothing I can do to harm you—"

"Frig you, shut up!" the saloon owner snarled. And then there was a series of fast, muted sounds that Edge was unable to identify. And Crowell instructed: "On your way, stranger! This ain't none of your business!"

"Thank God!" the preacher blurted, obviously becoming aware of the half-breed's presence for the first time. "I'm an old man in desperate need of help! Won't you—"

"Damn you!" Crowell roared. And this was followed by a more concise series of sounds, metallic and instantly recognizable to Edge. The thumbing back of a revolver hammer. So what he had heard earlier was the drawing of the fancy Remington from the cutaway holster. Now footfalls hit the hard-packed surface of the alley at a run.

"Don't fire at me, Crowell!" the half-breed snarled, the part-smoked cigarette ejected from his lips by the force of the words as he took a backward step.

The crack of a gunshot, amplified by the confines of the flanking brick walls, rang out in unison with the final word. A cry of alarm—a match for the one the preacher had vented when he fell against the horse outside the saloon—followed the end of the running footfalls. The bullet ricocheted amid a spray of red fragments and dust off the corner of the candy store perhaps three inches into the alley from where Edge stood, right hand draped over the butt of his still holstered Colt. Something bulkier than a foot thudded to the ground a little further into the alley. Crowell cursed and recocked his gun.

Edge rasped harshly: "I warned you," and drew and cocked his Colt as part of the same fluid action. The swing away from the front of the store, out of the cover of its wall to become a dark silhouette against the moon-bright, white-painted clapboard of the school house across the street at his back, was an extension of the same move.

He could see nothing in the pitch black of the alley's depths. He had neither the time nor the inclination to care if the old preacher had the sense to stay down on the ground where he pitched before Crowell fired. He instinctively adopted a sideways-on, slightly crouched stance as he placed his feet firmly and streaked his left hand toward his right: which was fisted around the gun butt close to his belt buckle. His right forefinger squeezed the trigger to explode the first shot. And part of a second later the heel of his left hand began to fan the hammer. The six chambers of the Colt were emptied in less than half that number of seconds, while the barrel was raked to the left then to the right. If Frank Crowell got off a second shot, Edge was unaware of the sound of the report or the effect of a bullet thudding into whatever was in its path. What he did hear, as with an economy of motion he tilted his gun and half cocked it to turn the cylinder so that the empty shellcases dropped from the chambers, was a man dragging his feet and breathing laboriously. And whispering voices could be heard nearby, others raised in the distance.

"You sonofabitch, life was good, it was real . . ."

Frank Crowell had staggered to the point where the moon's light and its shadow fringed each other. He rasped the accusation at Edge through teeth clenched in a grimace of misery and pain while tears of lost hope coursed across his tanned cheeks from his no-longer-bright eyes. His light-gray suit jacket was holed and crimson-stained in three places—one at the belly and two at the chest. He was still holding his fancy gun in a slack grip low at his side, lacking the strength to raise it. He started to bring up his free hand, seeking the support of the alley wall. But then he died, his eyes staring fixedly at his killer's hands engaged in the chore of reloading the Colt. He dropped his own gun, folded double and started to twist to the side as he collapsed to the ground. Footfalls hit the same stretch of ground again, but moving along the alley away from Edge as he stooped to retrieve his cigarette. He heard the hurrying old preacher sobbing with fear or relief or maybe pain as he retreated through the shadows.

"Way of the world, feller," the half-breed said evenly, and a scowl showed on his face in the flare of the match struck on the butt of the reholstered Colt. "Just when we think we've got a good thing going, it has to come to an end. Sometimes a dead one."

Chapter Four

A woman yelled, shrill with horror, from the doorway of a small house beside the schoolyard: "It's Mr. Crowell! Mr. Crowell from the saloon has been shot by the stranger!"

Her screeching announcement signaled a raising of many voices in the immediate vicinity that moments before had been held down to fearful whispers. This body of strident sound became intermingled with that vented by groups of local citizens approaching from the northern end and midtown stretch of the street. There were many more patches of light spilling out from windows and doorways up there now. But close by where Edge stood over the crumpled corpse of Crowell, the lamps that had been lit were now doused. And nobody who was shouting or watching in silence from the adjacent buildings dared to venture outside their shelter.

From several miles to the north came the mournful wail of a locomotive whistle as the engineer of the delayed train announced he would shortly be hauling the string of freight cars into the Prospect depot. The geldings in the traces of the preacher's buggy, already disturbed by the gunfire and the clamor of voices, were once more spooked into a struggling bolt hampered by the dead weight they had to drag. And then they were driven to a greater degree of panic by two more gunshots, these fired by the town sheriff, who was at the forefront of the crowd running down the street, his revolver aimed skywards as he exploded the shots in an attempt to silence the pandemonium around him so that Edge might hear his demand to surrender.

But the two shots served only to draw all attention momentarily to himself. And in the next instant the cacophony was even louder: as other men drew revolvers to explode them into the night sky, then thunderously loud, the final traces of shock gone so that just anger powered voices and actions, when diverted attention was switched away from the sheriff to the mouth of the alley, where the black-clad stranger to town no longer stood over the corpse amid the discarded empty shellcases.

To reach the boardinghouse of Mrs. Cloris Doyle, Edge had to turn right at the far end of the alley and head across the back lots of the barbering parlor, a feed and seed merchant and then around the backyard fences of two single-story houses. There was a mean-sounding dog chained up in one of the yards but nobody came outside to check on why he was barking and snarling as the half-breed slowed his loping run around the corner of the fence and closed with the rear of the narrow, three-story high boardinghouse. A just-starting-to-leaf shade chestnut tree, with some rustic outdoor furniture, on the back lot of the place, enabled Edge to reach a partially open window on the second floor. The important branch got to be dangerously slender where it reached toward the target window. And it sagged and creaked enough to erupt sweat beads of tension in the wake of those of exertion as he almost failed to get a handhold on the sill in the crack below the lower frame. Then his weight was transferred to the more solid support and he was able to push up the window so it was fully open, and snake himself headfirst into the room.

Then he closed the window and took a second or so to scan the night vista to either side of the tree's spring foliage. He saw the dog, just whining his frustration now, was as big as he had sounded. He did not see the emaciated old preacher or anybody else. Now he became aware of feminine perfume permeating the atmosphere of the unlit room. But it was a former presence this revealed, for he was alone, in the room and, he sensed as he stepped out onto the landing, in the house: for the whole place had an empty feel to it. But Edge did not trust such an intuitive response and allied stealth with haste as he went up the narrow stairway and into his room on the third floor at the front, where he took his gear from the closet and left without pause to glance ruefully at the clean and comfortable bed. Nor did he bother with the window for the muted body of sound now being vented by the angered citizens of Prospect indicated they were still concentrated in the area of the alley between the candy store and the barbering parlor. And he knew the angle was such that he would not be able to see that far along the street without opening the window.

By way of two flights of stairs, two landings, a hallway and a kitchen, he reached the back door of the boardinghouse. It was locked and bolted while the front one stood wide open in the wake of Mrs. Doyle and her other boarders crowding outside to discover the cause of the gunfire and the shouting.

The locomotive whistle sounded from much closer as Edge, his saddle and accoutrements over his left shoulder and his packed bedroll under his right arm, halted at the street end of the broad alley between the boardinghouse and the town bakery, from where he had a restricted view of an empty stretch of Prospect's main street and could see the full length of the just as deserted side street that formed a right angle on the west side—starting between the stone church with its pointed spire and the clapboard livery stable and hayloft of Joel Slocum. He was in deep moonshadow, but needed to cross something like a hundred feet of dangerously bright street to get to the temporary haven of the building where his gelding was enstalled. If everybody from this area of town had gravitated to the scene of the killing, no one was closer to him than a hundred yards or so, Edge judged. And if he was spotted, even if just before he made it into the livery stable, that distance did not give him enough leeway to get back out of the place in good shape to have a better than even chance of escaping this town unscathed.

He rejected with just a few moments of consideration the only alternative method of getting to the livery—circling some distance to the south and crossing the trail out among the homesteads. This would take too long and in the meantime the townspeople would have abandoned impulse for reason. The fact that he had taken his stuff from his room would have been discovered and his horse—and everybody else's, too—would surely be put under guard.

Maybe he could steal a mount from one of the homesteader's barns out in the country and . . .

"Brothers and sisters—friends—nobody but I alone is to blame for the violent end of that unfortunate soul!" the old preacher shouted.

And his voice was instantly recognizable, even though the words reached Edge from a considerable distance off. Just how far, he saw when he risked leaning out into the open to look around the corner of the boardinghouse as the skinny, dishevelled, gaunt-faced oldtimer continued:

"The keeper of the den of iniquity was driven by sinful impulse to further take issue with me for speaking of the word of Almighty God in his establishment!"

He was beyond where the main body of people were clustered on the street between the schoolhouse and the alley where Crowell's corpse lay, standing on the footboard of his buggy, holding his Bible in both hands thrust out in front of him—toward the angry and frustrated men and women who, albeit unthinkingly, were drawn to gaze at him by the mere power of his rhetoric.

"With God on my side, how can I fail?" Edge growled as he stepped clear of the moonshadow, to move without undue haste along a direct line from the corner of Mrs. Doyle's boardinghouse to the side street façade of Joel Slocum's livery stable, for the most part not looking where he was going, his face bathed with the sweat of high tension turned to the side; glittering eyes peering at the rear of the preacher's main audience, at the old man himself who was clearly visible up on the buggy, and the scattering of smaller groups and individuals on the street and the sidewalks and stoops beyond the speaker. These townspeople, not a part of the crowd, presented the main danger to the half-breed: that while they were held briefly spellbound by the commanding voice of the man on the buggy, they might glimpse on the periphery of their vision the figure moving far down at the southern end of the street.

"—and so I beg you, good people of this fair town, in the name of—"

Like many of the other listeners at closer quarters, probably, Edge for the most part heard the sound of the preacher's voice without paying sufficient attention to take in the sense of what he was saying. Then, as the half-breed reached a point a little past midway to his objective, the engineer of the behind-schedule train sounded another blast on his whistle that was loud enough to mask the old man's words. Instinctively, all eyes now switched the direction of their gaze. And Edge quickened his pace, to reach the livery and make the cover of the church before the preacher lost his audience in the wake of the whistle breaking the spell.

The melancholy sound faded from the night and was replaced by the muted but steadily rising roar of steam power. The old man tried to reestablish himself as a focal point, but no more than half a dozen words left his lips before he was cursed and howled and snarled into silence. At least, Edge assumed the preacher was the target of the anger because as he let himself into the livery and struck a match to get his bearings, there was no swelling of the tumult to indicate the vengeful crowd was surging down the street at the instigation of somebody who had seen him before he ducked out of sight.

He shook out the flame after seeing the stall in which his horse was quartered. Then he worked quickly but without undue haste to ready the gelding for riding; not so involved with the chore that he failed to keep listening to sounds from beyond the confines of the livery. First the again fading hubbub of angry voices, and then the rising volume of noise from the train became increasingly dominant as it slowed toward a halt in the depot at the far side of the town. Finally, the squeal of applied brakes, the clatter of cars one against the other and the gushing of excess steam from safety

valves acted to mask everything else to the ears of
Edge, even the clop of the chestnut gelding's
hooves as he rode the animal at an easy walk down
the center of the west-running street, which was a
street of stockyards and commercial premises, dark
and empty and closed up for the night, or, he
corrected himself as he saw the rundown and de-
cayed state of the buildings and the pens on either
side, closed up and shut down forever. It was a
derelict and ugly monument to the kind of town
Prospect once had been before the sodbusters moved
in on the surrounding country and proved the land
was better for growing crops than grazing Long-
horns. Better in terms of short-term profits, anyway.

Then he rode beyond the leaning post with the
broken crosspiece that once proclaimed the west-
ern limit of the town. And started out along the
open trail that gradually swung to the north of due
west as it rose up a gentle grade then cut through a
timbered ravine in which there were many signs
that it was the area where Prospect people came to
cut fuel for their fires. Maybe in the old days
building lumber had been taken from here, too. It
was many years since cattle in any large numbers
had been driven along the trail, for brush had a
tight and strong hold on the soil close in to either
side.

Beyond the timbered section of the ravine, he
struck another match and relit the part-smoked
cigarette that had remained angled from a side of
his mouth since it went out as he climbed the
chestnut tree behind the boarding house. Then he

dropped the dead match to the ground before demanding an easy canter from his mount: unworried that, after daybreak, a posse headed up by the most incompetent lawman west of the Red River would be able to pick up his tracks. Not that he was about to underestimate a man of whom he knew nothing, but it seemed a safe bet that a peaceful country town like Prospect certainly did not require, and probably did not have, the best sheriff in the state of Texas. And it was a good bet, if not a sure thing, that the kind of peace officer who wore the tin star in a town like that would not feel confident enough of his tracking ability to attempt the task at night.

So, believing he had the time element on his side, the half-breed now set about making an ally of distance. And he was certain he had doubly frustrated pursuit—with distance and then care to cover his trail as he zigzagged and backtracked, circled and where possible rode along water courses—when he saw the smoke of a small fire two nights and a day and a half after he secretly left Prospect. He was eating a noon meal of jerked beef and sourdough biscuits washed down with water without getting out of the saddle when he first glimpsed the dark smudge on the sun-bright blue above the distant heat-hazed skyline. Since he had never lost his bearings while he took pains to confuse possible pursuers, he knew he was still to the northwest of Prospect, heading today in a northeast direction. That meant the railroad spur that connected the town with the main Atchison,

Topeka and Santa Fe track bisected the terrain somewhere in front of him. So his first notion on seeing the smoke was that it came from the stack of a locomotive. But later he saw the source of the smoke was not moving and he rejected the idea of a stalled train for the more likely explanation that somebody had lit a cooking fire to prepare a more elaborate lunch than he had eaten.

The smoke was gone from the sky and there were just gray, cold ashes in the circle of stones where the fire had once burned when the impassive-faced, tense-behind-a-veneer-of-cool-composure half-breed reined his mount to a halt, in the mid-afternoon shade of a strangely eroded rock outcrop. He remained in the saddle as he raked his narrow-eyed gaze over an unfinished adobe building with a collapsed timber roof, an untidy scattering of unused building supplies, a diamond-shaped arrangement of eleven adobe grave markers and, parked beside the gleaming rails of the train track, a dilapidated buggy with two doleful-eyed, sway-backed grey geldings in the traces.

From within the building that had fallen into disrepair before it ever came close to being completed, a familiar voice called:

"Bless you, my son!"

Edge sent a globule of saliva into the burnt-out ashes and growled: "I didn't sneeze and my Pa's dead, preacherman."

Chapter Five

EDGE swung down from his saddle and led the gelding toward the open end of the building as the emaciated, ragged old man came carefully out, picking his way between the debris of the fallen area of roof. The lower part of his frock coat was dustier than the rest of his clothing from where he had been kneeling. He clutched his hat in one hand and his Bible in the other.

"Mock if you must, friend. I would ask that you do not, but I am unable to censure a man to whom I owe so much. Welcome to the Chapel of the Rock of Jesus. My name is the Reverend Austin Henry Loring."

"Edge," the half-breed replied, even-toned in contrast to the old man's fervor, and impassively unresponsive to Loring's toothless grin. "If anybody owes anybody anything, it's me to you, feller. But I don't plan on paying you back by lending an ear to your preaching."

The old man put his hat back on and took a

firmer, two-handed grip on the Bible; like he expected Edge to make a surprise snatch at it. "Whatever you wish, friend, sir, Mr. Edge. I fail to understand how you can be in my debt, but . . . ." He shrugged his shoulders, then became eager again after the moments of perplexity. "I was about to move on after my period of meditation. But I think now I will remain. You will rest and share a pot of coffee with me?"

"Sounds good," Edge answered as he unfastened one of his saddlebags, and removed a burlap sack which he set down on one of the stones encircling the dead fire. "I'll supply the grounds, you do the rest."

"As I said, friend, sir—"

"Edge is fine."

"Edge, then. Whatever you wish."

The half-breed led his horse from the outcrop into a patch of shade where there was a little scrub grass on which the animal could chomp. Then he hobbled him with a rope, took off the saddle and gave him a drink of water out of his hat. By this time, Austin Henry Loring had built and lit a fire with debris from the derelict building for fuel. And he had taken what he needed for coffeemaking from under the rear seat of his buggy. Edge climbed onto the buggy and drove it into the shade of the rock, on the other side of the building from where his horse was hobbled, and between the wall and the well-ordered arrangement of grave markers.

"Oh my, I've neglected them again," the preacher said with a contrite tone and a woeful expression. "I'm afraid I'm so often engaged in contemplation of how I may minister to the spiritual needs of my fellowman that I sometimes overlook the welfare of God's other creatures."

"Yeah," Edge acknowledged as he scanned the weed-choked burial area with the uninscribed markers at the head of the eleven mounds. Then he recrossed to where the buggy had been halted, wheelruts and hoofprints showing it had been driven here from the south, along a route that paralleled the railroad track just a few yards to the west of the twin curves of sun-glinting metal. Also stretching into the heat haze of the south—and into the north, also—along the same arc as the railroad was a line of poles with the telegraph wire strung between them. On the pole beside which the preacher had reined his buggy team to a halt, a wanted flyer had been tacked, freshly printed and not long enough posted to have been bleached by the sun or torn by the wind.

"Yes, I already knew your name," the old man said, still penitent.

"Yeah," Edge murmured again as he finished reading the bold, black lettering on the parchment-thick rectangle of cream-colored paper.

WANTED FOR THE

MURDER

OF

FRANK CROWELL

IN PROSPECT, SUN

COUNTY, TEXAS.

EDGE

Beneath this was a badly drawn portrait that did not resemble him in the least and a reasonably accurate physical description. Then came the request that information connected with the crime and its perpetrator should be communicated with the law office in Prospect. And finally, like it was an afterthought, mention was made of a "very generous reward."

"Sheriff Milton Rose had two hundred and fifty of those printed," Loring continued as Edge took out the makings and began to roll a cigarette. "And put up all over the county. I think he halfway believed what I told him about how the victim was killed. But he's a servant of the people who elected him to his office. And the dead man was very highly regarded locally."

Edge peered out across the rolling, low hill country scorching under the hot Texas sun, his mind given free rein to dwell on another time, far in the past, when wanted-for-murder flyers had been posted on him. But this memory and a myriad others it used to trigger remained locked up in a back, dark recess of his mind. And then, as he lit the cigarette with a match struck on the pole beneath the new flyer, he experienced a stab of ice-cold anger at the pit of his stomach. That threatened to expand and trigger a physical response when Loring added:

"The way you left town did not allow the sheriff to put his case for moderation very forcefully, Edge."

Between that old Kansas flyer and this one, he had killed more men than he was inclined to ever count, and rode away from the scenes of fatal violence without the law posting wanted notices on him. Maybe a desire for vengeance was even today still eating like acid on the insides of countless men and women who had lost loved ones at the killing hand of Edge. That knowledge he could live with. But being wanted by the law in a capacity that went beyond the jurisdiction of a here-today-gone-tomorrow posse was something entirely different.

But he confined the outlet of his ill humor to the way in which he arced the dead match into the air as he turned away from the vast vista east of the railroad. Then he did a double take at a portion of the outcrop close to the top, his eyes cracked to the narrowest of glinting slivers at the contrast between shadow and the brilliantly blue sky above.

"Ah, you have seen Him!" Loring exclaimed in almost frenzied excitement. "You have seen from the most perfect of viewpoints the face hewn into the solid rock by God's natural elements! The face of His son which I saw from that same spot so long ago! And felt called upon to commence building the Chapel of the Rock of Jesus!"

There was most certainly a similarity to a human face in the way the limestone had been eroded a little below the highest point, the eyes and the nose and the long beard of a man plain to see, just the suggestion of flowing hair where the rock was shaded darker than the surrounding area, and a misshapen and too large ear.

"Of course, in God's world—in His universe—nothing remains unchanging except for His abiding love!" Loring proclaimed as Edge moved back to where he had set down his saddle and other gear over the ledge of a glassless window in the chapel wall. "The wind and the rain or the dust it carries had done much damage to the image during the years between when I was first drawn here to the rock and when I had amassed sufficient funds to commence the building of the chapel! Fifteen long years, friend! And now seven more years of His weather have ravaged . . ."

He had come down from the high plane of zealous excitement as he watched Edge get a tin mug from the center of his bedroll and then come to squat on a block of crumbling adobe at the non-smoking side of the fire under the coffeepot: and knew his words were falling upon inattentive, if not deaf, ears.

"I'm sorry, Edge," he went on after the pause. "I vowed I would not speak of my convictions, did I not? But it was just the way in which you appeared to be drawn to look up at—"

"Weather does all kinds of strange things to all kinds of country, feller," the half-breed cut in. "Rock and sand, rivers and trees, mud and dust. Flames and clouds, too. I ain't normally in a frame of mind to pay much attention to that kind of thing. Was thinking of something else just then and seeing that face-shape up there gave me a jolt.''

Neither was Edge normally so forthcoming about his thought processes or so quick to volunteer the reason for an action he took. And now it was as if he was equally uncharacteristically perturbed by the way he had allowed his defense to drop: gave more attention than was necessary to the simple chore of pouring himself a mug of coffee, then offering to fill the old man's cup. Then the two of them, the half-breed seated on the adobe block and Loring on his feet, drank in silence for perhaps a full minute, each of them lost to the other in deep, brooding thought, until the preacher broke the morose silence.

''The man you killed was one of the four who did the killing here, Edge.''

''Yeah?''

''Ten converted-to-Christianity Indians and Norah. My wife of thirty months.''

The half-breed came out of his reverie and glanced back over his shoulder at the burial place, then looked at Loring, who nodded absently and sank stiffly into a cross-legged posture on the ground. He set down his chipped china cup at his side and seemed to withdraw again into a realm of melancholic private thought as he peered fixedly into the heart of the fire. While with one hand he held steady the fabric of his ragged frock coat the fingertips of the other one ran back and forth over an area where a tear had been darned long ago.

"Seven years in the past," he went on in a monotone voice. "On a day not unlike this. Earlier in the afternoon. The man you killed and three others. Red, Barr and Ben. We knew Crowell only by his given name. They were offered the hospitality of our camp. But they shot the Indians. Drew their weapons and shot them down in cold blood. Laughing as they did so. Then they intended to have their lusting way with my wife. But Norah denied them. By killing herself. But they were to blame. They forced her into such an act. She was young and very beautiful. Near a lifetime younger than me. I was left alive. Stunned by a blow to the head, but more than this."

He had abandoned his almost erotic fingering of the repaired rent in his coat. And now, as his tone began to get harsher and his gaunt, heavily-bristled, dirt-grimed face started to display a scowl of vicious hatred, he drew the battered Bible from a pocket; grew calm again as he clutched it tightly to his chest.

"When I recovered my senses, it was to find myself stripped naked and lashed by ropes to the naked body of my dead wife. Just a matter of feet away from me, vultures were tearing the mortifying flesh off the bones of the Indians."

He shrugged his skinny shoulders and shifted his gaze from the fire to Edge; showed no reaction to the cold impassivity with which his story of brutality and horror was being received by the half-breed who by infrequent turns sucked smoke from his cigarette and sipped coffee from the mug.

"The human mind is sometimes beyond the understanding of its host," Loring went on. And this produced an almost imperceptible nod of agreement from Edge. "Had the four men merely rendered me senseless before they rode away, I am sure my first impulse when I recovered would have led me to do as Norah had done. I would have found a weapon in one of the wickiups and ended my life. But the longer I was forced to endure my predicament, the stronger became my resolve: that if I survived, I would set aside my faith and seek vengeance."

"You want me to apologize for stealing your thunder back in Prospect, feller?" Edge asked, in the pause, while the preacher put away his Bible and took up his cup of coffee.

Now Austin Henry Loring's wasted face displayed a remarkably gentle smile as he shook his head very slowly. "Oh, no, Mr. Edge. I denied my faith for two nights and a day while the carrion vultures and the coyotes fed off the Indians, and the flesh of Norah decomposed beneath me. Before a train came by and my situation was seen. And relieved. My rescuers wanted to do more than merely release me, but I thank God I had sufficient strength to send them on their interrupted journey. For while I took the time to be restored to full health and then laid to rest by Christian burial my wife and my Indian brothers, my faith was returned to me. And was stronger than ever it was. I knew beyond a shadow of a doubt that it was not my perogative to exact vengeance for the atrocity committed here. 'Vengeance is mine; I will repay, saith the Lord.' This was the text of so much of what I contemplated in the aftermath of what happened here beneath the Rock of Jesus, Mr. Edge.''

Again he exchanged his cup for the Bible. But merely for the sense of security which he derived from holding the book now, as the smile that had faded from his shriveled face returned. ''Had I gone with my rescuers and allowed others to attend to what was needed here, I am certain I would have attempted to usurp the Lord God's right to vengeance. And had the faith of a lifetime irreparably shattered. Whereas I saw the true light and was able to see that I must change direction. The Rock of Jesus needed no man-made shrine, for it is sufficient unto itself. I had to do as I did before I came here. To travel far and wide and preach the Gospel to those following the paths of sin. Without need of worldly money to—''

''You're starting to sound like a preacherman again, preacherman,'' Edge cut in on Loring. First he tossed his cigarette butt into the fire, then the dregs from his mug and unfolded to his feet as he said: ''Obliged for the chance to rest up awhile. And for a lever I can maybe use to help me get out from under a murder rap.''

''Whatever I can do, you have only to request of me!'' the old man offered eagerly, thrusting the Bible back into his pocket and grimacing with the pain from stiffened joints as he struggled to rise.

"You told the town sheriff all that you just told me?" Edge asked, taking the hobble off the gelding's forelegs.

"Oh, no."

"You didn't?" He took the saddle off the window ledge and settled it over the back of the horse.

A rapid shake of the head, accompanied by an earnest expression. "It's none of his business, Mr. Edge. You plan to return to Prospect now?"

"Sometimes I go where I'm wanted," the half-breed answered with a wry, fleeting grin, as he straightened up from fastening the cinch beneath the belly of the horse.

The smile that spread across the filthy and withered face of Austin Henry Loring was toothless but shining-eyed, expressing joy held on a tight rein. "I must come with you!"

"You're wanted there, too."

"Oh, no, Mr. Edge. It was accepted by Sheriff Rose and everybody else that I was an innocent party in the death of—"

"Wanted there by me, preacherman. As a material witness."

"Oh, yes, I see . . ." The smile that had begun to slide from the gaunt features was now firmly back in place again. "You may rest assured that I am fully aware of my duty toward you. From the moment I looked out from the Chapel of the Rock of Jesus and recognized who you were, I knew our lives were to become inextricably entwined, for as long as it will take you to complete the mission you have been called upon by Almighty God to undertake.''

"If He called on me, feller, I must have been out at the time," Edge growled, moving to douse the fire with dirt after Loring had taken off the coffeepot.

"Mock if you must," the old man allowed, and showed just a mildly rebuking expression in the wake of the smile and just before he displayed a quiet brand of self-satisfied confidence. "But what the Lord God has ordained must surely come to pass." He hauled himself up onto the driving seat of the buggy and concluded: "When He demands a service, His will be done.''

Edge swung up astride the gelding and eyed the preacher bleakly as he replied: "It's your kind who perform the service after my kind have been by, feller. Funeral.''

Loring released the brake lever and clucked the sorry-looking gray geldings into motion, nodded and appeared even more composed than ever as the buggy drew level with where the half-breed sat on his stationary mount and said: "I have four of those in mind. Now that the Lord's instrument of vengeance has been shown to me.''

"You're crazy, preacherman!" Edge rasped, cold anger threatening to erupt to the surface again as he heeled the gelding forward and spat a globule of saliva sideways into the once-more-dead ashes in the circle of stones.

"You'll see. I've never been shown a clearer-to-read sign.''

The rider drew level with the buggy and drawled with no hint of irritation: "You haven't got a prayer, feller."

"I have an endless supply of those, Mr. Edge," Austin Henry Loring countered evenly, and perhaps with a trace of a smile.

The half-breed took a few more seconds to suppress the impulse to what he was then able to regard as groundless anger, as he glanced at the oldtimer driving the buggy, then said: "Instrument of vengeance, uh?"

"I am sure of it."

"And all you have to do is pray?"

"The wise are content to do what they are best at, don't you agree?"

"I've sometimes been known to bring other people to their knees."

"I'm sure that you do what you are best at most meticulously, Mr. Edge."

The half-breed vented a short sigh and growled: "Yeah, you might even say religiously."

Chapter Six

THEY followed the railroad track and prints left by buggy and team on the outward trip from Prospect, and in the unstrained silence of private they thought for several minutes, until Austin Henry Loring said in a tone of indifference:

"He was going to kill me. We each knew who the other was the moment we saw each other in his establishment. I was stunned. In a daze. I know I kept my wits about me sufficiently to leave and wander away from that . . . that place. But I have no recollection of doing it, Edge. My mind is a blank until I felt the man take hold of me and thrust me into the darkness of the alley. Where he demanded to know what I wanted of him."

The old man in the shade of the buggy roof glanced at the younger one astride the gelding a few feet to the side, saw that he seemed to have a greater degree of interest in the empty country all around than on what was being told him.

But the half-breed revealed he was listening when he said into the pause:

"And what was that, feller? Before your guardian angel of death happened by?"

A frown took a hold on the gaunt face for a few moments as Loring considered taking issue with the choice of words. But then the skinny shoulders beneath the threadbare frock coat were shrugged when one pair of ice-cold blue eyes met the rebuke expressed by another pair of similar color and overpowered it.

"As God is my witness, since I recovered from the evil that possessed me in the immediate aftermath of the savage violence at the Rock of Jesus, I never once contemplated revenge, Edge. Perhaps it was made easier for me to sustain such a tolerant attitude toward the wrongdoers because I never anticipated that I would ever see any of them again. When I did take a path that led me . . . well, as I said, I might just as well have been as senseless as when the man Frank Crowell and his partners in infamy left me to die. Then, when I was shocked back into a state of comprehension, I swear I experienced only pity for the man whose burden of guilt was compelling him to commit cold-blooded murder yet again. Only pity for him. Fear for my own life, I freely admit. And I pleaded with him and prayed to Almighty God to spare me. That my prayer was answered is without doubt a sign.

"I did not recognize it at once: was too filled with joy that my wretched life had been saved.

And I scuttled off into the darkness like a craven coward. But then I saw you making preparations to escape the unjust consequences of your act in coming to my assistance, Edge. Heard, too, the vengeful talk of those who were ignorant of the true character of the man Frank Crowell and would have perhaps punished you there and then if they had been able. So I sought to help you in some small measure by attracting the attention of—''

"Said I owe you, feller."

"*You* owe *me*? After you took a hand to save my—''

"Maybe he took the shot at you," Edge cut in again, rolling a cigarette as he continued to maintain an effortless vigil on the rolling hill country that spread to the heat-hazed horizons on all sides. "But he was talking to me. And the bullet was fired in my direction. I figure it was my skin I was protecting."

"I think—''

"I don't give a shit what you think about it, preacherman.''

"I intend to do what I can to have you exonerated of the crime of which you are accused, Edge," Loring said with rasping determination.

"You sure are."

"And you will then consider yourself more deeply in debt to me, no doubt?"

The half-breed struck a match on his Winchester stock and lit the freshly made cigarette. He answered on a trickle of tobacco smoke: "I ain't figuring on the people of Prospect setting much store by two strangers telling the same tale, feller. Even if the local lawman did halfway believe it when you told it. Going to have to flush out one of Crowell's old buddies, I guess."

A smile began to displace the quizzical look on the sunken and wasted features of the grizzled old man and became even more firmly set there when the half-breed cautioned:

"But I don't kill people for other people, preacherman. Not for money and not to repay a debt. Plan to bring in one of the other three to tell what Frank Crowell was a part of back there seven years ago." He jerked a thumb over his shoulder to indicate the distant outcrop with the unfinished chapel in its afternoon shadow. "Far as I'm ready to go for you."

"I am content," Loring responded, and seemed to have trouble in keeping his happiness within the bounds of the smile. "The Lord's will be done."

Another lengthy silence intruded between the two men as the hooves of the horses clopped, the wheels rattled and the timbers of the buggy creaked, while Austin Henry Loring continued to smile his satisfaction with the arrangement, and Edge maintained his effortless surveillance over this piece of Texas in which they were the sole human inhabitants, his impassive expression offering no clue to how he felt about the situation. And it was the older man who once more curtailed the agreeably undemanding peace, as the half-breed arced the cigarette butt into the dust. He said:

"I believe Sheriff Milton Rose to be a fine and fairminded lawman."

"If he's that, he'll be ready to take a hand in an old crime. When I make it his business."

Loring remained unperturbed by the implied reproof. He allowed: "Yes, I did say that, didn't I? But when I was still in Prospect following the death of the man Crowell, I could see no further than you as the instrument chosen by Almighty God. As that instrument, you will be guided by Him and—"

"I figure no more than twenty miles between the outcrop and town, preacherman," Edge interrupted.

"If more, not many."

"Somebody rode out that far to post the flyer on me. Trains come and go by the rock. Between Prospect and wherever. Some people on one of those trains seven years ago knew what happened there and—"

"I understand what you are saying, Edge," Loring cut in. He had reached into the back of the buggy and brought up a canteen, now sucked some water from it while the half-breed waited patiently for him to go on. "You have been out West for a long time, I'd say?"

"Since right after the end of the war."

The preacher nodded, briefly sad-faced, as he replaced the stopper in the canteen and returned the canteen to the back. "I, too. Many thousands of others. Ah . . . but I am leaving the point. With so much experience, you will understand how it could have happened—the growth of the town and the indifference to what took place at the Rock of Jesus."

The driving of the buggy required little attention, the two geldings in the traces sensing that unless a movement of the reins indicated otherwise they were required to follow the gentle curve of the railroad track. And the man in control of the reins held them very slackly in his hands which rested in his lap. Now he kept hold of them with just one hand while the other moved so that the bony fingers with the split and filthy nails could again tenderly explore the ancient darn in the frock coat. This as Austin Henry Loring went on in a neutral tone that matched his expression:

"Back then the town was nothing more than a few animal pens and a cluster of buildings erected by the ranchers and the men who built the railroad. Nobody even lived there for any length of time. Just at roundup when the trains came down from the north to load the cattle. Never was an economic proposition, but back in those days, cattlemen got to be very rich and railroadmen thought they could not fail to make money wherever they laid track. You must have seen similar crackpot schemes, Edge?"

"Yeah, guess so."

"Yes, I suppose bringing the materials for the chapel to the Rock of Jesus was the only contract outside of shipping cattle the Prospect and North Texas Railroad ever had back then. But I'm getting off the point again. The people who discovered me in such dire straits were aboard what might very well have been the final train to make the round trip from the north to Prospect. For they were going to town to wind up their business at that end. There was just not enough money in cattle to keep the company in business.

"Oh, dear, I fear I am being very long-winded about this? Perhaps making too much effort to stress that I blame nobody for turning their backs on the slaughter?"

"No sweat," Edge said in response to the implied questions and the inquiring look the old man directed at him.

"Nevertheless . . . the railroad people had their own troubles; if Prospect had ever been a town of any sort it then ceased to be so; and I moved on to preach the word of God far and wide." He sighed and followed this with a shrug. "Some Indians had been massacred and a beautiful young woman married to a cranky preacher more than thirty years older than her had killed herself. At a place which, after the railroad failed, was in the middle of nowhere. And where nobody came. Well . . . no disrespect intended, but to a man such as you . . . ?"

"Yeah, feller," the half-breed acknowledged after he had taken a drink of water from one of his own canteens. "I hadn't figured on Prospect being so new."

"Best part of seven years," Loring explained. "Since the first group of homesteaders moved onto the land down there."

"You were through this part of the country between seven years ago and just the other day, preacherman?"

A vigorous shake of the head as the sun inched

close enough to the southwestern horizon and lost enough heat so that the veil of shimmering haze was almost neutralized—and a just discernible pall of woodsmoke became visible in the far distant south: formed by that which wisped from many chimneys in Prospect.

"No, I never was. In truth, I did not even realize where I was until after the fury following the shooting had died down, and I had given my account of what happened in the alley to the sheriff. You see, I have traveled whatever path I have been guided along by Almighty God since I accepted my new role in His service. Never feeling the need nor the inclination to question where I was nor where the next path would take me.

"After the sheriff and his posse had set off in pursuit of you as dawn was breaking, I felt drawn to the town church. For once to seek guidance in the light of circumstances, after I had given thanks for my deliverance and offered up a prayer that you might escape cruel injustice. Day was fully broken and the sun was risen when I emerged from the church, Edge. And in daylight I could not fail to recognize the old buildings and animal pens, disused now, that I had first seen . . . well, there had been just too many signs to be ignored. I asked a few questions of the liveryman who had tended to my team and then straightaway left town to follow this railroad to the Rock of Jesus. Where, I must admit, my faith in you as an instrument to direct the wrath of God began to suffer setbacks: as time elapsed and you were not guided to me. But then . . . all is now well."

Edge looked at the old man for the first time in several minutes and saw he had abandoned his fingering of the old mend in his coat and had once more taken the battered Bible from his pocket, was clasping it tightly, and yet again seemed to extract some kind of force from the book that added light to his dulling eyes, color to his wan flesh and strength to his flagging frame.

"We'll rest up beside that clump of brush over there, preacherman," the half-breed said, and it was obvious from the way he started that Austin Henry Loring had been totally absorbed in deep contemplation as he received the spiritual refreshment that had such a marked physical effect upon him.

"Oh, I feel I could travel for eternity, my friend!" the old man exclaimed eagerly, and looked fervently at Edge after casting a dismissive glance at the patch of greasewood, mesquite, mulberry and poison ivy at the start of a gentle incline.

"I get too close to town before dark, feller," Edge growled, "eternity will likely get started for me from the end of a rope."

"Oh, yes. Of course. What do you have in mind to do?"

"Go on living free."

Austin Henry Loring bobbed his head in enthusiastic agreement as he halted the team alongside the saddle horse reined in by the rider. He said: "Yes, of course. But I meant what do you intend to do in Prospect after it is dark, Edge?"

The half-breed dismounted and said wryly: "The way you tell it, preacherman, the will of God."

The old man became grave-faced as he continued to sit on the seat of the stalled buggy and gazed fixedly at Edge. He intoned: "I would urge you most earnestly not to mock, my friend. Almighty God is a just and merciful Lord but he is able only to help those who help themselves. And the only way—"

"I told you, preacherman," the half-breed cut in coldly. "Don't preach to me."

For stretched seconds Loring gazed as intently at Edge as Edge at him; and for the duration of this challenging confrontation, seemed on the brink of defying the command. But he abruptly dropped his gaze, and appeared drained, older than his many years and even sick. He found his Bible was temporarily out of recuperative power and shoved it sullenly back into the pocket of his frock coat before he climbed unsteadily out of the buggy. Even his voice sounded feeble when he asked sadly:

"Have you no faith at all, Edge?"

"In myself, feller."

"I know there is a God on high," the oldtimer countered, and moved to take his team out of the traces as Edge unfastened the saddle cinch. "And whether you are prepared to accept it or not, I know He made all of us in His image."

"Some of us Friday nights."

Chapter Seven

THE irreligious man called Edge and the devout oldtimer named Austin Henry Loring ate a cold meal of biscuits and beans washed down with stale canteen water as the afternoon moved into evening. Then, as the sun sank with a change and softening of color from yellow to pink through red, the half-breed dozed with his hat tipped over his face and the older man gave silent study to his Bible. One of them sprawled on his back with his head resting on his saddle, the other seated so that his back leaned on a wheel of his buggy.

The hobbled horses moved a little and made muted noises. There was reverence in the delicate and almost silent manner in which Loring turned the pages of the book, and finally closed it when the light was too bad to read by anymore. Which was when, almost as if he had been awakened from a light sleep by the muffled sound, Edge came up from the ground and set his hat back on his head.

"Time for us to leave?" The old man sounded weary still, and totally lacking in the fervor that had sustained him during the afternoon drive from the outcrop.

"No, feller," Edge answered as he peered to the south, where a dull aura of light in the night sky had supplanted the smoke pall of late afternoon to mark the position of Prospect. "Time for me to leave. You stay here."

"Why?" he asked, neither looking nor sounding overly interested in getting a reply.

"Because you can use the rest?" Edge suggested as he picked up his saddle.

"I can't deny it," was the equally indolent response as he fisted the grit of strain from his sunken eyes. "How long do you want me to remain here?"

"Until I get back."

"But how am I to know? Anything could happen to you. You could . . ."

The skinny shoulders were shrugged and the haggard face expressed apprehension as he watched Edge prepare the chestnut gelding for riding. In the soft light of the moon, it looked as if there was a gentle mockery in the smile of the half-breed as he swung up astride his saddle and said into the pause left by the unfinished sentence:

"I thought you were a man of faith, preacherman?" There was nothing gentle in his tone.

"In God. May He go with you."

"Obliged," Edge said, and touched the brim of his hat with a forefinger as he tugged on the reins to move his mount in a slow wheel. "You just keep it in mind that He moves in some mysterious ways, uh?"

This encouraged the oldtimer to bring a weary smile to his toothless mouth and unshining eyes. He countered: "If I did not constantly keep reminding myself of that, Edge, I would on countless occasions have abandoned the path of righteousness to step onto the slippery slope that sends the sinful plummeting into the fires of Hades."

"Don't know how long I'll be gone, feller. But try to keep cool, uh?"

He heeled the chestnut gelding forward at an easy walk between the telegraph poles alongside the railroad track, and was conscious of the preacher peering after him with solemnity or perhaps even dejection in his sunken blue eyes, while Edge was content that he had gone as far as he was willing to go in offering the oldtimer peace of mind. Then, when he had ridden to the crest of the long slope and no longer sensed the somber eyes staring fixedly toward him, he was able easily to put all thought of Austin Henry Loring out of his own mind, and to keep his memory confined to serene inactivity and his conscience from disturbing him without too much effort while he watched the night-veiled country on every side of him: and paid particular attention to the south, where, minute by minute as he made slow progress following the line of the railroad track and the accompanying wire-strung poles, the town of Prospect could be seen in more detail from a viewpoint he had never taken before.

At first, as he rode onto a discernible trail past the most outlying of the homesteads, there was just the pitched- and flat-roofed skyline of the distant cluster of buildings under the fringe glow of the light from many windows. Most of the homesteads scattered among their carefully tended fields of newly sprouting crops to both the east and the west of the parallel railroad track and wagon-wide trail were already in darkness, the farmers and their families bedded down early to prepare for a dawn awakening. And as Edge closed with the town, the clop of the gelding's hooves from time to time causing a dog to bark, a horse to snort or a cow to moan, the citizens of Prospect began to take to their beds. And the aura of light emanated by kerosene lamps began to fade as window after window was darkened to leave the buildings as black silhouettes against the star- and moonlit country to the south.

He saw that it was not just an association of ideas that had caused the preacher to sermonize about being drawn toward Prospect by the narrow cone of the church spire. It truly did provide an ecclesiastically dominant marker on which even a secular stranger could home in. But then Edge spat, a little irritably, into the dust, recalling that he had paid no more attention to the church spire than to any other aspect of the town when he first approached Prospect from the south. And anyway, he was no longer a stranger and needed no kind of

marker in order to get a bearing on where he knew
he was going.

At the town-limits sign that was in a better state
of preservation than the one on the west trail into
Prospect, Edge reined in the gelding and for perhaps ten stretched seconds scanned his surroundings in every direction before he swung fluidly
down from the saddle. Not a single sliver of artifi-
cial light competed with that of the moon and stars
out in the homesteaded area of the country. Almost complete silence had a seemingly palpable
presence in the cooling air of near midnight, kept
from being absolute by a faint and ever constant
rustling of stray wisps of breeze among the fields
of young crops. In town, an occasional crack of
light showed where a door or a drape did not fit
properly in the frame, or at a window where somebody could not sleep, did not want to yet, or was
afraid to with the light out. There was a body of
sound from among the buildings—a low hum comprised of the countless indistinct and often unidenti-
fiable noises made by any large group of people
undergoing the involuntary processes of staying
alive while they slept. Restive movement contributed to the sound, but the half-breed saw nothing
that moved along the deserted length of the broad
main street before he led his horse over the railroad track into the shadowed cover of the depot
buildings.

He hitched the reins to a strut of the framework
that supported the timber water tank and went the
rest of the way on foot, watching and listening for

the first sign of danger—but reasonably confident that his instinct for being watched was not letting him down. He moved stealthily but with self-assurance between the cover of the railroad depot to the rear of the telegraph office that was back on the other side of the track, and the trail: the first building on the west flank of the street's northern end.

Had his resolve to finish what he had started been blunted for any reason during the measured approach to Prospect, it would surely have gotten honed sharp again by the wanted flyers posted on the railroad depot and the telegraph office façades—and doubtless on other public buildings throughout town. The flyers were identical to the one tacked to the telegraph pole out at the outcrop Loring had named the Rock of Jesus. But these had a more recently printed strip pasted beneath them, emblazoned in large lettering:

REWARD NOW $3,500 DEAD OR ALIVE.

All was darkness and quiet in back of the telegraph office, a line of stores and the office of *The Prospect Tribune* which Edge had to pass to get to the rear of the Best in the West saloon. Between the newspaper office and the saloon, behind the false front of what would otherwise have been a six-foot-wide alley, was a darkly moonshadowed outside stairway that gave access to the upper storys of both buildings.

He took care to set down his booted feet quietly

on the open treads, but was unable to avoid the timbers creaking under his weight. And within the close confines of the flanking walls the stressed planks sounded like they were screaming loud enough to wake everyone in town and out in the country. But Edge was familiar enough with the tricks a man's mind can play at times of tension to be able to recognize this as one of them: so he stayed poised to respond instantly to any aggressive move against him without looking for danger where it could not possibly be.

On the open landing behind the false front at the top of the flight of stairs, he first tried the door to his left that gave onto the second story of the newspaper office building. It was not locked. And neither was the door that faced it across the landing in the side of the saloon, which made his task that much easier and which he did not consider either fortunate or odd: people who lived in quiet country towns where strangers were a rarity were as likely to leave doors unlocked as locked.

The brief flare of a match had shown him what he wanted to see beyond the first door he opened. He went without a light across the threshold and onto the second-floor landing of the Best in the West, closed the door at his back and waited a few seconds for his eyes to get accustomed to the lower level of light inside. And light there was: that of the moon that filtered in through the net curtains hung at a window at the far end of the landing.

He moved toward this window that looked out

onto the roof of the single-story stage line depot
that abutted the saloon on this side. He did not go
all the way to the window at the head of the stairs
that curved down into the barroom which was
redolent with stale tobacco smoke, body odor,
perfume and strong liquor. Instead, he halted at the
last but one door on his left. He knew this gave onto
the room from which the blond-haired and scantily
dressed Marsha had called down to the soon-to-die
Frank Crowell three nights ago.

His stealthy footfalls had counterpointed the deep
breathing and rasping snores from behind several
of the doors as he moved along the landing from
one end almost to the other. He could hear nothing
from beyond the door he now opened—until it was
wide enough to allow him to step through. She
was sleeping peacefully and breathing easily, on
her back with her hair spread out across the pillow
at either side of her face which did not look so old
in the flattering light of the moon that shafted
between the drawn-aside drapes at the window.
The fact that she was in repose and, from the
sweetness of her breath, had not been drinking
before she came to bed probably aided the moonlight in making her look younger.

Edge reached the side of the bed in two and a
half long strides and did not use time in contemplation of the attractive features of the woman
in the framework of spread hair; nor the well-
proportioned length of her body and limbs ap-
pealingly contoured by a single sheet that made
it obvious she was again wearing only the flimsiest

of night attire. The moment he came to a halt, he drew the Frontier Colt but did not cock it. He transferred it from his right to his left hand, then back to his right, but this time fisting it around the barrel. Then, without the slightest sign of a grimace or even the blinking of an eyelid, he thudded the base of the butt against her left temple at the hairline, hard enough to sound a muted crack of metal hitting bone with just a thin cushion of tissue between. The skin split and a little blood seeped from the fissure as the woman's head was wrenched to the side by the force of the blow. She made no sound to indicate a conscious awareness of pain: but curtailed her breathing for several moments. Then she began to breathe more deeply than before.

The half-breed slid the gun back in the holster, peeled the sheet to the foot of the bed and could not fail to see that the nightgown she wore was sheer enough to reveal the dark areas at the base of her belly, crests of her breasts and at her armpits. Elsewhere her skin seemed to be as pale as the color of the diaphanous gown. There was a natural gentleness about the manner in which he stooped, raised the unconscious woman into a limp, seated posture and then folded her over his left shoulder—like he was taking precautions about causing her any further discomfort. Then, as he straightened up and turned and carried her out of the room, he ensured that her body and limbs were as decently covered as the daring nightgown allowed and took care to keep her firmly in position without touching her intimately.

And he continued to treat the insensible woman with the utmost decorum until he had carried her out of the Best in the West and into the second-story pressroom of *The Prospect Tribune*, carefully closing each door behind him. There he set her down on the nearest available chair with no consideration for her posture or modesty while he spent something over a minute familiarizing himself with the workings of the flatbed handpress in a corner of the room. He discovered how to raise the heavy platen high up off the bed so that he could slide out the form of type from beneath it. Then he unfolded the hinged tympan to free the form, which he was careful to set down gingerly on the floor even though he recognized it as the setting for the reward rider to the wanted flyers on him. He took as much care to be as quiet as possible in shifting the lightest table in the room to position it end-on to the press. Then he slid the bed without a form on it back under the platen, and again observed the proprieties in picking up the senseless woman and lowering her, face up, onto the table, with her head resting on the bed of the press. Next he checked that the see-through fabric of her night-gown was pulled high at the neck and low at the ankle-length hem and at the wrists, before he worked the bar handle to lower the spring-pressured platen until it just touched the tip of her nose.

Then he vented a sigh of satisfaction and took the time to make and light a cigarette. He held the flaring match at the same level as the gap between the platen and the bed to keep the darkness at bay while he double-checked what he had achieved, grunted his dissatisfaction and, in the moonlight entering through grimed and dusty windowpanes, made some adjustments. He raised the platen, turned Marsha's head on the side and worked the bar to narrow the gap once more, not so much that she would feel any pain from the pressure when she regained consciousness; but sufficient so that she would not easily be able to pull her head clear.

He sat down then, after dragging a chair to the side of the press and leaned forward from it to put his face on a level with that of the woman. He started to smoke the cigarette at a faster than usual rate, not inhaling, and blowing out the smoke from pursed lips into the face of the unconscious woman, who, before the cigarette was smoked down to half its length, came coughing and gagging back to awareness. At the start of this, Edge dropped the cigarette to the floor and crushed out its fire beneath the toe of a boot.

The hand that had dropped the cigarette now moved into the hair at the nape of his neck and emerged as a fist around the handle of the razor, which he carefully pushed toward the throat of the woman, whose terror at coming awake to the sensation of choking had almost instantly been subdued by agony from the blow with the gun butt, then a moment later was displaced by greater fear. And her mouth gaped wide to vent a scream when she found she could not move her agony-filled head. But just a whimpering moan sounded when the cold metal of the flat of the razor's blade was pressed to the sweat-tacky flesh under her jaw. And then she caught her breath as a match was struck, its flare blinding her for a moment before she saw the lean, glittering-eyed, darkly-bristled face of Edge.

"Three choices, lady," the impassive half-breed told her evenly.

She started to breathe again and he had to ease the razor away from her to keep from slicing into her flesh when she swallowed hard before she rasped: "You're the man who killed Frank."

"All three and a half thousand bucks worth of me, lady."

"I can't move. Where is this? What are you doing to me?"

Edge shook out the flame before it burned his finger and thumb and dropped the match as he replied: "Make the right choice and nothing more that's bad will happen to you. Far as I'm concerned. You're in the press room of the local newspaper next door to the Best in the West. Make one of the wrong choices and I'll cut you dead. Make the other—"

"Please, mister, I—"

". . . the other wrong choice," the half-breed concluded levelly, "and I'll leave you flat."

Chapter Eight

MARSHA was looking her age again, as the throbbing pain inside her skull mixed with the chilling terror that had an icy grip on every fiber in her body: this combination acting to contort her face and deepen the lines in her cold-sweat run skin.

She was probably still on the right side of forty, but only just, with a firm and statuesque body that was standing the test of time better than her face. It was an oval-shaped face with regular features that in the best of circumstances after a skilled application of the right shades, paints and powders would more than merely hint at the classical beauty the woman had possessed as an innocent young girl; before the passing years and loss of innocence took a toll.

Her teeth were still good, white and evenly matched as she clenched them in determination not to give in to panic. And, even at this moment of nerve-twisting tension, there was beauty in the round, wide, thickly-lashed eyes of the woman.

"First wrong choice is to start to scream, lady," Edge told her evenly. "You'll drown in your own blood from a cut throat before you finish it. Second one is act the dumb blonde so I have to put the pressure on you. Best to tell me what I need to know and that way your headache won't get any worse."

"Please, mister," she hissed through her gritted teeth, and now closed her eyes tightly. "You murdered the man I was going to marry. Frank's dead so there's nothing you can do to cause him more harm. And I can't understand. Why do you want to cause me more suffering than you have by shooting him down like some mad dog you'd cornered in a—"

"Okay, lady. The way you dress for bed I couldn't help but see you ain't a true blonde. And I've heard enough to know you're not dumb. All you have to—"

"This is crazy. Like a nightmare. My whole world is getting turned upside down." There was a tremulous shrillness in her voice and her eyes began to emanate a hard glitter as she moved toward hysteria.

"I have nothing against you, lady," Edge said.

"It looks like it," she countered, taking a grip on sullen anger to combat the urge to panic.

"Had nothing against Frank Crowell until—"

She snorted now.

". . . he took a shot at me when I told him not to. It was one for one, Marsha. Self-defense."

"You should get together with that crazy old

preacherman, mister. Get the stories you tell into line. He says you gunned down Frank to keep him from killing—''

''Austin Henry Loring told me about that, Marsha. It's what he honestly believes happened and—''

''I don't want the murderer of the man I was going to marry calling me by my given name, mister!'' she cut in, and now it was a brand of righteous indignation that sounded in her tone and showed on her pale face in the ink-smelling darkness of the flatbed press. ''My name if you have to call me anything is Miss Onslow.''

''He told me about what he thought happened in the alley down the street, and a great deal more, Miss Onslow,'' Edge said, not entirely certain that her abrupt switch to this new mood was a step away from hysteria. ''Mostly about something that happened seven years ago. Did you know Crowell that long?''

''Having this knife against my throat is scaring the shit out of me, mister,'' she said. Paradoxically, she sounded calmer.

''You don't have any plan to yell for help, Miss Onslow?''

Now she proved she was self-composed enough to have thought rationally about her predicament. And his. She replied: ''I'm no brilliant mind, mister. But I'm not dumb the way you were talking about it a while back. No, I don't have any plans to scream. Start squeezing my head under here though and I won't be held to any promise you figure I've made. And I reckon the whole damn town will be here to ask you some questions before you've squeezed me—''

He withdrew the razor and returned it to the pouch at the nape of his neck. He said into the pause that followed her unfinished sentence: "I was asking if you and Crowell had a long engagement, Miss Onslow?"

"You're not going to release me from under this thing?"

"No."

"So we can talk like two civilized human beings?"

"I'm not much of a talker, Miss Onslow. But I'm going to tell you what Austin Henry Loring told me. You ready to listen?"

"I have any choice?" she countered sourly.

He told her the bald facts about the massacre at the Rock of Jesus. He referred to the place by the preacher's name for it just once and did not name the four men who committed the atrocity until he concluded: "Frank Crowell and three other men did the Indian-killing and then left after Loring was lashed to the corpse of his wife, Miss Onslow. One of the others was named Barr. And there was a feller called Red and another one who was Ben. I need to find at least one of those three, Miss Onslow."

The story of the seven-year-old tragedy had been told in not much over a minute, during which time the woman had gasped and caught her breath on several occasions, the grimace of horror taking a firmer hold on her features at each sound she vented in response to the coldly spoken words of the impassive-faced half-breed. After which, he patiently waited out a pause of perhaps half a minute; not attempting to anticipate how Marsha Onslow would seek to counter the allegations against her newly dead fiancé, but mildly surprised when she ended the silence by saying:

"Yes, I can see how Frank could have been capable of such a thing back then. And it explains his phobia about anything to do with religion and the church. Especially how he just couldn't abide to have a minister near to him."

"Not asking you to allow that Crowell took a hand in what happened out where the church was being built seven years ago, Miss Onslow. Need to know if those three names I mentioned mean anything to you."

"They were his friends," she replied in the same dull-toned voice: her manner vague as if only one small part of her awareness remained in the newspaper pressroom while most of her consciousness was concerned with times and places far removed from her. The new assault of shock and the horror it triggered had been reduced to a numbing effect on her capability to experience any kind of emotion to the present circumstances. And she was maybe fitting into a fresh pattern, events during her relationship with Frank Crowell that she had never before been able to slot into context. "They were in the war together. Not proper soldiers for the CSA. Frank was part of some group . . ."

"Raiders?" Edge suggested, satisfied with the line Marsha Onslow was taking.

"Yes, that's right. Somebody or other's raiders were what they called themselves. Don't ask me for the name. Red and Ben and Barry I only remembered because you reminded me."

"Barry?"

"Barry, Barr . . . whatever. I've known—I knew—Frank since a couple of years ago when I first came to this town and he gave me a job as croupier on the Best in the West roulette wheel. We got to be pretty close pretty quick and in two years people who work and live under the same roof all the time say a lot to each other. Talking is about all there is to do in towns like Prospect, mister. The kind where the most exciting thing to do most times is to go down to the livery and watch the horses shit."

"No Indians to shoot up, preachers' wives to rape—"

"I've heard about a bunch of savages getting killed out at a place where the fallen down church is, mister!" she snapped, fully back in the present again now. "Like most strangers to town who arrive by train, I saw the church and the grave markers. And I asked about it. Not Frank, because I was here in Prospect a few days before he gave me the job and I'd already had my curiosity satisfied by then. The way it was told me—and the way it's told to any other stranger around here who troubles to ask—nobody knows how the savages and the woman came to be shot up the way they

were. Because the old man who was fou.
the corpse of the woman was crazy out
mind. Sent those who found him on their v.
And had buried the dead and gone his own way
the next time people went by the place.

"You say it was seven years ago. I don't know.
Just that it all happened back when this town was
no more than stockyards and a railroad depot for
loading cattle into cars. Whatever, Frank was a
drifter back then. Him and the three guys he came
west with after the war was over. He told me
about that time in his life every now and then.
Mostly when he drank too much. And that didn't
happen very often. But he never spoke of taking
part in anything like what happened at the chapel
beside the railroad, mister. That is the honest truth.
Mostly he only spoke about the past since he came
to Prospect in the early days of the town and how
he built the Best in the West from nothing. Then,
after we were engaged to be married six months
ago on the twentieth coming, we spoke mostly
about the future we would have together. Turned
out to be a lot of talk about nothing, didn't it?"

She sniffed and Edge altered his opinion about
the reason for the light that entered her eyes while
she was talking in the dull monotone. It was not
triggered by tightly controlled anger. Marsha Onslow
was on the brink of spilling tears of despair.

"Just Red, Ben and Barr or Barry?" he posed.
"Crowell never used their—"

She sniffed again and swallowed hard. And her
determination not to break down sounded in the

severity of her tone when she answered: "I've told you, mister. I probably wouldn't have been able to tell you those names. You reminded me of them. It could be that if you told me their other names, I'd be reminded again. But I just don't know if Frank ever called them Smith or Johnson or whatever. All I do know for sure about anything is that I'm reaching the end of my tether, mister."

"I believe you, lady," Edge told her.

"You better believe me, mister," the woman rasped back at him. "Because although I don't want to get my throat slit or have my head crushed, I can feel a scream coming on. And I don't know if I can stop it."

"Much obliged for the warning," he said, and rose from the chair. He heard her gasp as the bar squeaked faintly when he shifted it; then she caught her breath and held the scream in check when he moved the handle so that it eased the platen up off the side of her head instead of pushing it lower. "And for being so honest with me," he added as he turned away from the press when he saw she would be able to withdraw her head and get clear of the machinery and table on which she was sprawled as soon as she felt capable of doing so unaided.

"You wouldn't have taken the risks of coming back to town if you didn't believe in what you are trying to do, mister," she said, after she had moved just to the extent of rolling her head so that she was staring up at the underside of the platen. "Knowing Frank the way I did I can believe as wholeheartedly as you that he did what you claim. He's dead and I could have been. What point in lying?''

''None, Miss Onslow,'' he answered from close to the door, half turned toward her as he reached for the handle.

''Nor in you saying you're sorry for mistreating me the way you did? After you misjudged the kind of person I am?''

''Right, no point,'' Edge told her as she continued to lay along the table with her head in the press, only her scantily covered torso moving with her measured breathing as her tone of voice suggested her mind had wandered into the maze of the past again.

He pushed open the door and stepped sideways across the threshold and onto the landing at the head of the outside stairway, then pulled the door closed. He froze with his right hand still draped to the handle of the door when something small and hard and circular was pressed against his spine, midway down his back. And a man's voice he failed to recognize growled:

''I can tell you more about one of Frank Crowell's old wartime buddies, Edge. Why don't we go—''

The half-breed powered into a counterclockwise turn. He kicked off with his right toe and gave impetus with a shove of his right hand against the door handle. This as he spun on his left heel and whiplashed his left arm backwards. Thus was he only a quarter way through a full turn when his rigid left forearm impacted with the hand gripping the revolver and dislodged the muzzle from against his spine.

"Sonofa—" the man holding the gun started to rasp into the void that followed what he had been saying before.

Then Edge reached the halfway point of a full turn: his right foot and his fisted right hand swinging with greater speed than his body. The foot hooked behind one of the splayed legs of the surprised bushwhacker an instant ahead of his fist crashing into the side of the man's jaw. The man's gun hand thudded against the door of the newspaper pressroom and the revolver slipped from the pain-slackened grip. Then the man's shoulder and his head hit the same door, powered there by the force of the punch. Next he was sent staggering across the landing when Edge completed the full turn, propelling the man with the foot hooked around the back of one of his ankles.

The half-breed had barely glimpsed the man as he whirled to counter the act of having a gun muzzle jammed against his back. He saw fleetingly in the dark shadows of the neighboring buildings and the false front of the alley as his punch landed that the man was almost as tall as himself, guessed he was a great deal lighter from the way he started to go down from the blow. He only realized just how slightly built the man was as he crashed off the landing and started to bounce down the stairs in a confusion of flailing arms, flying legs and twisted torso. He was as stringbean skinny as Austin

Henry Loring and, just for one hallucinatory moment, Edge was gripped by the insane thought . . .

But then the man, having uttered no cry of pain or alarm as he clattered clumsily down the open-tread stairway, came to a spread-eagled halt on the hard-packed ground at the bottom, face up, with his top half clear to see in a patch of moonlight—some of which glinted on the five-pointed star pinned to the left breast pocket of his shirt.

There were some confused sounds from within the Best in the West. Then the door on the other side of the landing was wrenched open and Marsha Onslow vented a strangled cry of pain as she stepped across the threshold.

"Oh, shit!" she snarled as she stooped to pick up what her bare foot had stepped on, and came up holding the Army Colt that had fallen out of the grasp of Sheriff Milton Rose.

Edge plucked the gun from her hand while she was still scowling at it for causing her injury, and murmured: "Obliged again, Miss Onslow."

She scowled at him now, then glanced down at the unconscious man at the foot of the stairs and did a double take. She gasped: "Holy cow, it's Mr. Rose! What happened?"

"I don't like having a gun aimed at me."

"He could have fractured his skull, falling all the way down—"

"If he did, it should be a neat fracture," Edge cut in as he started down the stairway, while the muffled voices and muted footfalls from the Best in the West rose in volume.

"What are you talking about, mister?" the woman demanded wearily, exploring the blood-crusted and bruised area on her own head.

"He was a sucker to brace me the way he did, lady. And I always try to give a sucker an even break."

Chapter Nine

MARSHA Onslow got the door of the newspaper press room closed before the one across the outside landing was wrenched open and a man with a sleep-thickened voice growled irritably:

"Goddammit to hell, Marsha, what's all the noise?"

Edge was in a crouch to pick up the sheriff's hat from a tread midway to the foot of the stairway. The lawman's gun was in his free hand and he made to swing it up to aim at a target. It was not cocked when he took it away from the woman and now he just rested his thumb over the top of the hammer without clicking it back.

A little light reached feebly out over the threshold after spilling along the inside landing from a lamp in one of the rooms on the second floor of the Best in the West. And the shadow of the man who complained the loudest at being woken up further diminished the level of light that fell onto the woman in the diaphanous nightdress. But it was sufficient to clearly show the scowl that remained firmly set on her no-longer-beautiful face as she continued to explore that injury at her temple. She scratched it now, though, instead of gently massaging the discolored bruise so that her fingernails scraped off the congealed crusting of old blood and drew fresh, liquid crimson from the split in the skin. Then, with the eye on the blind side of the spokesman for the complainers, she winked at Edge and lied:

"It was about me falling down the lousy stairs, Wilbur." She moved forward, into the open doorway. "Stepped outside for a breath of air. Couldn't sleep on account of thinking so much about Frank lying dead down at the mortician's parlor and—"

Men and women began to make sympathetic noises while others expressed concern about the blood on her face. But what they were all saying and the conclusion of Marsha Onslow's invented explanation for the disturbance was abruptly reduced to an incoherent murmuring when the woman closed the door, and the outside stairway was once more shrouded in moonshadow.

Edge let out his pent-up breath and turned as he straightened. He pushed the lawman's gun into the waistband of his pants at his belly and carried the dislodged hat down to its still unconscious owner, where he fixed the Stetson in its proper place by using the chinstrap before he lifted the man and draped him over a shoulder. He carried him behind the newspaper office, the stores and the telegraph office and then across the end of the street and the railroad track to where the chestnut gelding was hitched beyond the depot.

It was no great strain for him to carry the tall and skinny Sheriff Milton Rose, who did not weigh more than a hundred and sixty pounds; and was so flaccid in unconsciousness he might have been boneless. It was equally easy for the powerfully built half-breed to fold the lawman face down over the saddle on the gelding. He did not tie him there. He led the horse at a slow walk that did not threaten to upset the slumped balance of the oblivious Rose and paid scant attention to the shallowly but regularly breathing man. Instead he maintained a cautious watch on the almost silent and not quite entirely darkened town that was huddled to his left as he half circled around the northwest side—to get onto the little-used trail he had taken the first time he needed to leave Prospect secretly. But Marsha Onslow's playacting had apparently been a genuine effort to help him get clear of town, for he reached the timbered ravine through which the west trail cut without an alarm being raised.

Here he called a halt after leading the horse off the gently rising trail and into a clearing among the timber on the south side where the night air was redolent with fresh sawdust. He hitched the gelding to a low branch of a young pine and lowered the unconscious man to a patch of turf—on his back with his own hat to provide a pillow of sorts. Then he sat down on one of several tree stumps and rolled and lit a cigarette. Still he devoted less attention to Rose than to watching for a first sign he had been followed from Prospect, until, shortly after he crushed out the cigarette butt beneath a boot heel, Milton Rose groaned back from unconsciousness and snapped open his eyes.

They were dark-colored eyes in a dark-stained, leather-textured face. His thinning hair was darkest of all. His teeth, displayed in a grimace of pain as he tentatively moved his limbs and eased his head up off his hat, looked extremely white by contrast, like those of a Negro. This was the first time Edge had cause to look carefully at Rose from close quarters and saw now that the man was a lot older than he appeared at a distance. He was close to and perhaps more than sixty.

"So your right arm ain't broken, feller," the half-breed said evenly.

Rose had been able to start thinking despite the pain and he clawed a hand toward his empty holster the instant he recalled why he was in such pain. Then, as the first word was spoken, he wrenched his head to the side; had to blink his eyes a number of times to bring the image of Edge seated on the tree stump into sharp focus.

"Nor your neck," Edge went on. "You want to try moving everything else?"

The grimace that had been displaced by a scowl now returned to the long and lean face of the lawman as he struggled to sit up and did a lot more blinking as he peered about himself.

"I get riled at having a gun poked into my back, sheriff. Like it even less than having one aimed at me. Cocked or not. You ever have cause to draw against me again, try to kill me. I sure as hell will be trying to kill you.''

Rose shook his head several times with his eyes closed, then opened them again and made a three-hundred-and-sixty-degree survey of his surroundings. There was confusion mixed in with the pained expression on his face now.

''You took a tumble down the stairway between the saloon and the newspaper office—''

''I've figured that out for myself, mister,'' Rose cut in.

''Fifteen, maybe twenty minutes ago. We're about a half mile out along the west trail from Prospect.''

Now the lawman nodded, and rasped between gritted teeth as he hauled himself up onto a tree stump ten feet away from where the half-breed sat: ''Thought I recognized this ravine.''

He remained puzzled until Edge explained: ''I had some help, sheriff. Marsha Onslow gave the people you woke up a good story to cover for the racket you made taking the tumble down the stairs.''

Rose nodded again, as he gently massaged the pained areas of his body and head, giving most attention to his crown and his right knee. He said in a self-satisfied tone: ''Yeah, it's about time that woman came to the good senses I always knew she had.''

''You lost me,'' Edge told him.

''If I can get together whatever good senses I got, I'll try to tell you what I was plannin' to say before you laid me out, mister. Which I figure I can't blame you for doin'. A man gets a gun

111

stuck in his back in a town where he's got no
reason to figure anyone sees things from his point
of view, he's just bound to get a mite mad. But
you gotta see my point of view on what I done,
mister.''

He abandoned ministering to his bruises and
hooked his bony hands over his angular knees as
he eyed the half-breed with a brand of odd-in-the-
circumstances repentance; like Edge was the wrong-
fully injured party.

''I do?''

''Yeah, you do. On account of I'm on your side
in this thing. And I'd like to lend you a hand to
sort out the mess. Same way that Marsha is root-
ing for you and helped you out. But you got no
reason to believe a word I say nor to trust me in
anything unless you see why I done—''

''Which of Crowell's wartime buddies can you
tell me about, sheriff?'' Edge interrupted.

''Not much about any of them. But most about
Barry Donovan.'' He said this very quickly and
then spoke even more rapidly. ''I don't sleep too
good these days. I got the insomnia that the doc
says there ain't no cure for unless I drink myself
into a stupor, which ain't of no interest to you. So,
anyways, I was wide awake and fixin' to start out
on my normal midnight swing through town when
I seen you ride into town off the north trail and
leave your mount in the cover of the railroad
depot. Recognized you from the way you move.
Don't get many of your kind through Prospect. So,
anyways, I seen you move on foot into town and

I'm real puzzled, mister. Way I seen the kinda trouble you took to shake off me and the posse out in open country. So I bides my time instead of roustin' out some help to get you locked up in the Prospect hoosegow. Seen you go up the stairway between the *Tribune* buildin' and Frank Crowell's place. Did some sweatin', I can tell you, mister. While I waited to hear a shot or somethin' that would've meant you'd killed somebody else. And I almost yelled up there for you to quit what you was doin' when I seen you carryin' the woman outta the saloon and into the other buildin'.

"But I'm real glad I didn't, mister. And that's no horseshit. After I heard you and Marsha Onslow talking. But, like I told you, I figured you'd be tensed up real tight when you stepped outta the *Tribune* doorway. Likely to lash out or worse when I opened my mouth to say somethin'—or if you just plain saw me before I had a chance. Reason I held my gun on you, and I sure hope you believe me?"

His tone of voice and quizzical expression made it a query.

Edge told him evenly: "No harm done, feller—to me. Donovan, Red and Ben?"

Milton Rose obviously was not fully satisfied with the response he had drawn from the half-breed. But it rankled for just a few moments, before he shrugged and sighed, and supplied without his earlier haste:

"Red Maguire and Ben Tremayne. I was a Texas Ranger when I had my dealin's with them as a

113

bunch of four hard men back from ridin' with Micky Rankinn's Rebel Raiders in the war. I rode up from the San Angelo ranger post to check out a rumor about some kinda massacre some place along the route of the Prospect and North Texas Railroad track. But just found what's to be seen there today, more or less. The grave markers and the church— not so fallen down, I guess. Some wickiups and some old sign that a wagon had been driven away from there. Along with a bunch of unshod horses. But this was eight weeks after the rumors said it happened, and there'd been no official complaint lodged. And since, most of the stories went, it was all redskins that were killed . . . well, anyways, even if I had set much store about a minister's wife bein' under one of the headstones . . ."

Milton Rose shrugged his skinny shoulders again: and was shamefaced as he remembered part of his seven-year-old past and realized that the passage of time had not made lame excuses any more valid.

"Prospect was just startin' to change from bein' a railhead for cattle shippin' to what it is today," the lawman went on, drawing himself back from the brink of self-pity. "The first sodbusters were ploughin' and sowin' on their claims and a half dozen merchants were startin' in to build stores. Frank Crowell and Tremayne, Maguire and Donovan were gettin' off the ground with what I guess was what was to become the Best in the West. In the old Cattleman's Association buildin' that ain't there anymore on account of it was burned to the ground when some oil lamps got busted in a big fight.

"There was a fight at the place almost every night. About a woman or a card game or just for the hell of it. Like I say, though, Frank Crowell and his buddies were a hard bunch and they could handle their own trouble. And they never did have any of the kind that gave the Rangers cause to have any kinda official interest in them. But I didn't like the kinda place they was runnin' in the kinda town that Prospect was tryin' to be. And nor did a lot of other folks that I guess you could call the foundin' fathers of today's town."

Edge took out the makings and started to roll another cigarette as Milton Rose paused: the sheriff seeming to need to take the time off from talking while his mood altered from depression to contentment in response to the more pleasant memories that crowded into his mind. But after he looked away from the infinity on which he had been reviewing the events of the past and saw the unencouraging lack of expression on the face of his listener, he felt it necessary to sidetrack:

"All this I'm tellin' you is kinda important, mister."

"When there's no rush, I'm a good listener, feller."

"There's no rush."

"There isn't?" Edge countered, and gave the lawman an up-from-under look as he ran the tip of his tongue along the cigarette paper.

Rose fleetingly smiled more brightly at having

produced a visible reaction in the naturally impassive half-breed, and supplied: "Barry Donovan
ain't scheduled to reach town until three-thirty
tomorrow afternoon, mister."

Now Edge showed a smile of his own. But from
the way in which Rose suddenly appeared nervous,
it was apparent the lawman saw the dangerous
glint in the ice-cold eyes that lit with no warmth as
the lips were drawn back from the teeth. But his
tone was easy when he said:

"Like I say, a good listener, feller."

"Sure. Okay. Where was I? Oh yeah, I was a
Texas Ranger when I spotted them four as trouble.
But they didn't cause none that I could take a hand
in as a Ranger. And I left to go back to San
Angelo. But I had it in mind to come back, mister.
See, I was nearin' the end of my time. And a
bunch of sodbusters and business people hereabouts—the decent ones that wanted Prospect to
become a fine and peaceable town . . . well, they
let it be known that if I was still interested in bein'
a lawman after the Rangers figured I was too old
for the service, they'd be happy to have me as
sheriff.

"Which is what I got to be, less than a year
after I was first up this way to look into that
business out along the railroad. Even though there
was precious little call for the place havin' a full-
time peace officer. Town was really startin' to
build up and there weren't no real flies in the
ointment. Like I told you, the first saloon and
cathouse and gamblin' place in the old Cattleman's

Association buildin' was out of business after the fire. And Maguire and Tremayne, who were the meanest of the bunch we're talkin' of, and Donovan, had all left these parts. Only Frank Crowell was still here and he was runnin' a plain and simple saloon.

"Didn't stay just that for long, though. Branched out into gambling again first. Then built another floor on the place and brought in the whores. But he always kept a tight rein on the place and I never had any call to visit the Best in the West on law business. Never was alone in figurin' there never should be a place like that in a town like Prospect. But Frank Crowell kept all the sinnin' out of sight behind the batwings of the place, he gave more than any other local businessman to the Community Chest and worked real hard to stay in the good books of even the folks who made no secret of how they felt about the kinda place he was runnin'. Just had this bee in his bonnet about the church and anythin' to do with the church. Couldn't abide to pass the place except on the other side of the street. Wouldn't come to any meetin' if the town preacher was gonna be there, too. And if he spotted a Bible or a crucifix or a rosary or any kinda religious thing like that in a room, either it went out or he did.

"So I figure you can start to see it from my point of view now, mister?"

"No, feller."

Rose expressed a scowl of irritation. "Rumor had it that four men did the killin' out along the railroad track. Crowell and his three buddies could've been by there at about the time it happened. One rumor said the wife of a preacher was included in the dead. And there sure was a church bein' built when the killin' put pay to it. Maguire and Donovan and Tremayne left this part of the country but Crowell stayed. Got to be as respectable as someone in his business can get, but never could clear his conscience, I figure. You gotta be able to see why I always had a strong notion Frank Crowell and his three buddies was the bunch that did the—''

''Can see that plain enough, feller,'' Edge allowed, and struck a match to light the cigarette he had been toying with for a minute or so.

''So you can see why I'm keen to lend you a hand to clear yourself? If at the same time Donovan and Mag—''

''What I can't see from your point of view,'' the half-breed interrupted again, ''is why Crowell was still alive and free to go gunning for Austin Henry Loring. And why his three wartime raider buddies are maybe in the same state of health and liberty if the preacher should happen to come by? When a peace officer had a strong notion—''

''That's easy enough for a man like you to say!'' Sheriff Milton Rose snapped, and came suddenly erect; in his anger of injured pride forgetting he was still suffering the effects of the tumble down the stairway. But he was able to hold back a cry of pain behind a grimace of anguish as his punished body protested the abrupt movement. And he almost stumbled, but was able to call upon a great strength of willpower to stay upright on widely splayed legs. "You're a free agent that don't have to pay any attention to the laws of the land if you don't want to! Nor even to what your friends and neighbors are likely to say and do about what you do! And what you can do is just about anythin' you damn well want! And if you get away with it, all you gotta do then is move on out to whatever business you got someplace else! Am I right, or am I wrong, mister?"

"Depends on a feller's point of view, I guess," Edge allowed, and there was perhaps just a flicker of warmth amid the glitter in the slits of his eyes as he showed an otherwise wry smile.

Rose remained at a high level of anger that acted to numb his pain for several stretched seconds. Then the fire in his dark eyes died and for a few more seconds he teetered on the brink of giving in to the demands that his ill-treated body made upon him. But he fought back the impulse to collapse into a heap amid the tree stumps and began to move slowly about the clearing. And he used talking to augment walking as therapy to dull the pain.

"All right, mister. A lot of what I been sayin' is crap. When I was younger and stronger and had a whole lot more pride than I got now, I was one of the best Texas Rangers in the entire state. Did most jobs the way the book said and when that wasn't possible, did them my way. Rangers never have been angels, mister. But I done my stint of livin' like you. When I left the San Angelo post

119

and got to be the peace officer at Prospect, I planned for it to be a kinda semiretirement. I wasn't so sick back then at the start as I am now, but what's been eatin' away at my insides for so long was already startin' in to feed.

"Can take that, mister. Got myself on terms with it on account of knowin' there ain't a damn thing I can do to stop it chompin' away at me until it bites into somethin' real vital and I have to go meet my maker. What I can't come to terms with is not doin' nothin' about that old massacre. Sometimes figured I was gettin' to live with it easy on my mind. But that was only when I never come across Frank Crowell for days at a time. Soon as I spotted him again . . ."

"You sure Donovan will be coming to Prospect tomor—"

"Appreciate it if you'd let me finish, mister," Rose cut in, moving in a freer gait and not grimacing now. He did not look at Edge for an acknowledgement and spoke quickly before the half-breed had an opportunity to voice a negative response. "When I heard about the preacher and Crowell . . . well, even though Lorin' didn't say so, I figured he was the one that was buildin' the church when the killin' . . . But I couldn't figure out how a man like you fitted in. And I had to go along with what the folks that pay me wanted. Raise a posse and take off after you. Did my damnedest to locate you, mister. Was real eager to find out about you and Lorin' and Crowell all bein' mixed in together. But you lost me and good. And when me and the posse got back to Prospect the preacherman was gone, too. So there wasn't a thing I could do except try to content myself with knowin' that Frank Crowell had paid at last for what I was sure he done out along the railroad all them years ago.''

''I'd say, sheriff,'' Edge growled as the tall, stringbean-skinny lawman halted a few feet in front of where he sat and looked down at him, ''that there's something else you have to say?''

Milton Rose's grin of self-satisfaction was briefly gone from his haggard face while he stooped to pick up his crushed Stetson. Then it came back and was brighter while he reshaped the hat and set it on his head, before he gave a slight nod and replied: ''Wasn't a thing I was able to do except try to content myself—and get off a wire to Barry Donovan sayin' that his old buddy Frank Crowell was dead and askin' him if he wanted to come to see the remains buried.''

Edge crushed the fire from his cigarette on the tree stump where he was seated and said: ''Obliged, sheriff,'' as he came erect.

''That all?'' Rose countered, surprised and vexed.

''You've already told me what time his train is due in at the Prospect depot tomorrow,'' the half-breed reminded as he moved toward his gelding.

''But I was gonna tell you about him, mister!'' Milton Rose blurted. ''How he's gone up in the world. Got to be bigger and richer than Frank Crowell. Runs the Donovan Freight Line Company outta Santa Fe. One of the biggest operations of that kind in the whole of the southwest.'' .

"Here," Edge said, and drew the man's Army Colt from the front of his pants waistband. "And remember what I told you to do if you have cause to aim it at me again. Either here, or when I bring Donovan to you and the rest of the townspeople and have him get me out from under the three and a half grand that's on my head."

He tossed the revolver at the lawman, who made no attempt to catch it as he again spoke rapidly into the pause left by Edge.

"Was gonna tell you about the reward, mister. And about how I figured somehow to get Donovan to tell me where Maguire and Tremayne are these days. And then there's Marsha Onslow you oughta know more about. And . . ."

His voice faltered and then faded as he watched Edge swing up astride the gelding after unhitching the reins from the branch of the pine tree.

"Guess you'll be able to walk back into town okay?" the half-breed asked, after backing the horse off the tree and bringing him around in a tight wheel.

"I ain't helpless!" Rose snapped sullenly with a scowl. But then he moderated his tone and showed a crestfallen expression when he added: "Exceptin' when it comes to doin' the chores Prospect folks hired me for."

"Something, feller," Edge said, reining his mount to a halt after the gelding had picked his way among the stumps to the trail.

"Yeah, mister?" the sheriff asked, ready to be

cheered, as he straightened from retrieving his gun which he now thrust back into the holster.

"Have it in mind to do this just for myself."

Now there was a mournful mixture of self-pity and bitterness on the gaunt face of the old and sick and in pain man. The five-pointed tin star pinned to the left pocket of his dark-colored shirt gleamed brightly in the moonlight as it moved with the rise and fall of his narrow chest in a sigh.

"But the way it's shaping up," Edge went on . . . "It looks like I could be striking a blow for law and holy orders."

Chapter Ten

THE train that was scheduled to reach the depot in Prospect at three-thirty was running late and, as he sat astride his chestnut gelding in the afternoon shade of the Rock of Jesus, Edge idly wondered if the funeral of Frank Crowell would be delayed to await the arrival of the train. He also pondered in the same indifferent manner upon the whereabouts of Austin Henry Loring, who had not been waiting where he was told when Edge returned to the clump of brush at the foot of the shallow incline after he parted company with Milton Rose in the ravine last night. He did not reflect at all on the Prospect lawman. He did, though, more than once consider with regret his missed opportunity to have Rose explain Marsha Onslow's seemingly inexplicable actions after he treated her so badly in the newspaper pressroom.

But none of these spontaneous lines of thought engrossed him very deeply. And the possibility that not one of the questions posed might ever be resolved did not perturb him in the least. He was merely filling time with any trivial notion that entered his mind while he kept effortless watch along the railroad track that swept away to his left and his right in gentle curves. Looking for the train in one direction and for whatever or whoever might appear in the other, he also did not ignore the vast area of apparent emptiness spread out on the other, eastern side of the railroad. The outcrop with the distinctively eroded face that threw a gradually lengthening shadow across the unfinished chapel and the mounted half-breed blocked to his view much of the country to the west.

Edge had reached the scene of the seven-year-old massacre a little before dawn and had bedded himself and his mount down in the section of the chapel which still had a roof—in need of this cover to protect himself and the horse from the direct heat and glare of the soon-to-rise sun rather than to keep out the chill of what was left of the night. He slept until noon and then laid and lit a fire on the dead ashes in the circle of stones. He cooked some bacon and beans and boiled up some coffee.

He was through eating by one-thirty and did nothing except sit on a block of adobe in the shade and maintain a casual surveillance over his surroundings for the next ninety minutes. Since he was judging the time by the position of the sun as it moved across the cloudless afternoon sky, he knew his estimates could be only approximate; and so he was prepared to be several minutes wide of

125

accuracy as he saddled and then mounted his horse when he calculated the train should appear at any moment through the heat haze that shimmered on the northern horizon.

He knew he was not almost thirty minutes fast, though, and as this amount of time drifted into history he gradually devoted an increasing amount of attention to the country which the railroad bisected to the south: looking for the first sign of a double cross—or maybe the second such sign if the failure of the train to show was part of a three-and-a-half-thousand-dollar sellout.

But then a smudge of blackish smoke appeared above the northern horizon where the blue of the sky shaded into the gray of the haze. And less than half a minute later the shimmer-blurred shape of the smoke-belching locomotive came into view. In back of the engine were two passenger cars, two boxcars, a flatbed and a caboose; Edge was able to see the makeup of the train as it came clear of the haze on the curve of the track. Just a few seconds after this, as the entire length of the train appeared in perspective to merge into a single unit, he realized the locomotive was being fired to hurtle south at great speed, which caused him to heel the gelding out of the shade and steer the reluctant and nervous animal over the closest rail and onto the ties earlier than he had planned—so that the engineer on the locomotive footplate had more than two miles in which to spot the man on horseback in his path.

The gelding did not like the feel of the crushed

rock of the railbed under his hooves and was happier when he was standing comfortably on two ties, facing north. But shortly after this the flanking rails began to hum with the vibration from the speeding weight of the approaching train. Edge stroked the animal's neck gently and spoke soft-toned nonsense into the pricked ears. The engineer sounded the steam whistle in a long blast of warning without making any change to his speed. When the shrill whistling sound was abruptly ended the hiss of high pressure steam, the thud of pistons, the rattle of speeding wheels and the clatter of metal on metal could be heard, initially muted by distance but swelling in volume by the moment.

Edge maintained the unhurried cadence of the stroking motion of his hand down the left side of the neck of the perturbed horse, but would have needed to shout to make himself heard above the noise of the advancing train which was now far enough around the shallow curve for just the cowcatcher, circular front of the tank, headlight and smoke-streaming stack to be seen by the composed half-breed and the nervous horse. And to yell would have defeated the object.

The whistle shrilled again. But for a shorter warning burst, before the screech of locked wheels along the rails was added to and became dominant among the cacophony of other sounds from the train. Showers of glowing red and yellow sparks sprayed outwards and died in the steam and smoke-tainted air to either side of the locomotive with the number two-oh-seven painted in gold on its green tank.

About five hundred yards separated the locomotive and the horse and rider. The horse's head came up and his lips drew back as he vented a snort of fear that could not be heard through the din. Edge knew his mount was intent on a rear and maybe a wheel on hindlegs to precede a bolt as the vibration from the rails was conducted along the ties and felt through the shod hooves of the animal. He had expected as much without being able to estimate when the horse would panic: could only hope it was after man and mount together had been spotted by the engineer, whose vision was surely impaired by smoke and steam and dust and sun glare—and who maybe only glanced out every now and then along the path his train was taking. This hope realized, Edge tensed to make a move of his own in relation to that of the gelding, but was icily calm in contrast to the equine panic. He withdrew his right foot from the stirrup as he ceased to stroke the animal's neck with his left hand. He clutched the saddle horn with the left hand at the same time as he let go of the reins with his right when he shot forward to fist around the frame of the booted Winchester. The horse was starting to go up into a rear then. Edge slid the rifle smoothly out of the boot as part of the same move that brought him upright on his left foot in the stirrup as his right leg swung up and over the saddle and bedroll. The horse wheeled to the right. Edge came off him to the left, powering himself clear with a push against the stirrup and the saddle horn that served also to urge the horse into a greater commitment to wheel and bolt—going clear of the man who half jumped, half fell to the railbed, his body and limbs held in a crouched attitude to absorb the impact that was painful but not bone-cracking. His toes came down on crushed rock and his heels on a tie. He tipped forward between the rails and his hands, the right one clutching the rifle, hit another tie. The screeching of locked, spark-spraying wheels along shuddering rails continued to dominate the whole discordant din of sounds from the rapidly slowing locomotive and the line of cars behind it, and to mask the thudding hooves of the gelding, which was a fading sound anyway as the spooked horse bolted in headlong panic away from the track on the opposite side from the outcrop and the chapel, while Edge was deaf to the obscenity he rasped through teeth gritted in a grimace as the jarring pain of his landing was more intense than he had expected.

But he fought against the debilitating effect of the searing sensation at his ankles, knees and left wrist, and gave an impression of being just a little stiff as he rose to his full height, with his legs slightly splayed, his left thumb hooked over the buckle of his gunbelt while his right hand held the Winchester canted casually to his shoulder. What this cost him in terms of willpower could be seen for stretched seconds in the strain that showed on his unwashed and unshaven face where every line seemed to be gouged suddenly deeper into the dark-hued flesh and every pore squeezed out an overlarge bead of salt moisture that coursed down the lines and got entangled in the bristles. But for as long as it took him, as a matter of pride, to rid his features of the distorting grimace and to stem the sweat of tension there was no one close enough to see him as he did not wish to be seen. Then, as the train came to a snorting, hissing, clanking, shuddering halt with the leading point of the cow-catcher less than twenty feet from where he stood, the half-breed could not be seen at all. For he was enveloped in a rolling cloud of steam from the escape valves and a billowing cloud of more opaque smoke from the stack of the locomotive.

The engine itself was also partially hidden within its own outpourings, which began to lessen at much the same rate as the sounds it emitted diminished. And Edge was able to hear what the two men up on the footplate were yelling at the same time as he emerged from the swirl of steam and smoke and saw them.

"—some crazy man on a friggin' nag, Larry!"

"—ain't doubtin' you, Orin! Yeah, I see the horse out there . . . shit, and there's the guy!"

"Stranger, you coulda been killed!"

"Sure coulda, mister! If Orin wasn't the best damn engineer in these parts! And he hadn'ta stopped this train better than I ever seen a train stopped before in an emergency!"

Orin was fat and angry. His much smaller fire-man was a kid less than half his age who was agog with admiration.

"Man that can't stop a train ought never to be allowed to start one, feller," Edge said as he moved by the footplate on the opposite side of the stalled train from the Rock of Jesus. "Passengers'll be glad to know the railroad only hires on skilled men to—"

"Sonofabitch!" the engineer snarled across the even-toned voice of Edge. "Where the hell you get off, blockin' the permanent way on this rail—"

Edge halted at the foot of the steps at the front of the day car coupled immediately behind the tender. He was aware of three faces with puzzled expressions on them pressed up against window panes to get a restricted view of what was happening outside and below. He also saw the uniformed brakeman climbing down from the caboose, with the movements of an old man suffering from stiffened joints.

"You'd have stopped if I'd just made a hand signal, feller?" Edge cut in on Orin, and dragged a forearm across his face: saw the blackness of soot as well as the dampness of sweat on his shirt sleeve.

"Damn right I wouldn't, stranger! I'm only supposed to stop a train at officially designated depots or when ordered to do so by a duly appointed official—"

"Rules are made to be broken," the half-breed growled as he climbed aboard the car, trying not to look as arthritic as the brakeman who was now hurrying with a limping gait alongside the train.

"Not when it puts human life at risk!" the

engineer snarled at Edge, whom he could no longer see because of the intervening tender with its high load of cordwood.

"Speaking of which," came the still even-voiced response from the platform of the first day car, "if you fellers try to move this train out before I tell you, it'll be your lives that'll be on the line."

Orin spoke a string of harsh-toned obscenities as Larry attempted to placate him and the brakeman started to yell that the train was already late and to demand to know the reason for the emergency halt. All of which Edge ignored as he opened the door and stepped off the platform into the car. He announced:

"Living's better than dying, I figure. Anyone wants to check if I'm wrong just has to try—"

He said this as he started along the central aisle of the car, addressing a scattered audience of seven nervous listeners comprised of a man, woman and little girl of about ten who had peered out of the window at him; two middle-aged men who had been playing cards together and an old man and a young one of about fifteen who were travelling alone.

"I ain't armed!"

"I just have a couple of dollars!"

"Don't hurt my daughter, please!"

"It's just trinkets, my stock-in-trade, sir! But you're welcome to take it!"

Some hands were thrust toward Edge as he strode down the aisle of the car, rifle still canted to his shoulder, thumb hooked over the uncocked ham-

mer and forefinger curled to the trigger. Those of
the man in the family group were splayed and
empty. One of the card-playing drummers offered
some screwed up bills and the other held out a
carpetbag, while the small girl reluctantly allowed
herself to be embraced by her anxious mother, and
the old man sat rigid and tight-lipped, tacitly challenging the half-breed to try to rob him. The acned
adolescent who was at the rear of the car, fixed the
rifle-toting intruder with a look of scorn and spoke
in a matching tone of voice as Edge came level
with him and pulled open the door.

"All I got is some candy, you crook. Real easy
to take that off a kid, they say." He thrust his
hands deep into his pockets, as defiant as the old
man.

"Candy, uh?" Edge posed after a glance across
the two platforms of the end-to-end day cars and
through the glass panel of the leading door of the
second one.

"Yeah!"

"So chew on it and don't talk with your mouth
full, kid. Could turn out to be a lifesaver."

He stepped out of the car and closed the door
beind him, muting the blustering voice of the boy
as he harangued his fellow passengers for not standing up to the half-breed. Then, briefly while he
stepped from one platform to the next, he could
hear the irate voices of the engineer, the fireman
and the brakeman, who were all now down off the
train—but remained in a group beside the locomo-

tive which became quieter by the moment as the boiler pressure fell.

There were just five passengers in the second day car. Another family group, but this couple's offspring was just a baby in the arms of the young woman. They sat just inside the doorway to Edge's right, the woman looking ready to faint with fear as she cradled her sleeping baby while her husband encircled her trembling shoulders with one arm and draped his other hand over the butt of his holstered Remington. This hand had white knuckles and shook, and there were beads of sweat on his forehead and along his top lip.

"Right now I don't want a thing from you or your missus or your baby, feller," the half-breed said softly, and did not even seem to look at the man again after an initial glance. "You don't let go of the gun and keep your hand clear, I'll take the lives of all three."

"He means it, Clyde!" the woman forced from her terror-constricted throat.

"I believe you, mister," the man added quickly.

"Belief is the same thing as faith, feller," Edge said, and continued to look toward the other two passengers in the car.

"If you say so, mister."

"And that can move mountains."

"That's what they say." He swallowed hard.

"Just want you to move your hand away from—"

Clyde jerked his hand up from the gun as if the butt had suddenly become unbearably hot. His wife vented a sob that disturbed her sleeping baby.

But he gave just a whimper before he settled peacefully again.

"Obliged," Edge said.

"You didn't leave me much choice."

"For not making me kill your baby."

The mother sobbed again and Clyde murmured
words of comfort to her. While the half-breed
moved toward the second couple who rode in this
car—seated at a midway point along the aisle on
the other, Rock of Jesus side, both of them dressed
expensively in black mourning, the woman in the
aisle seat, the man by the window.

The woman was a slender redhead in her mid-
thirties with a doll-pretty, blue-eyed and full-lipped
face. She looked to be as fearful of Edge as the
mother—clasped her hands tightly in her lap as if
to stop them from shaking and seemed incapable
of blinking while her gaze was apparently trapped
in a fixed stare at the impassive face of the half-
breed. The man beside her was half a head taller at
six feet and was much more broadly built; his bulk
composed largely of fat if the padding of flesh on
his round, smooth, pale-skinned face was anything
to go by. His eyes were also blue, but were much
smaller. And they blinked a great deal as one sign
of his nervousness. He was also sweating, and the
part-smoked cigar between the yellow-stained first
and second fingers of his right hand had gone out
from neglect. The constant movement of his tiny
eyes revealed that Edge was not the sole cause of
his apprehension. He was also disturbed by what

he was able to see through the dusty window of the car.

"You're Donovan?" Edge asked as he came to a halt and captured the same high degree of attention from the seated man as from the woman at his side.

Donovan attempted to voice a reply but was able only to vent an inarticulate grunt. He nodded and either the sound or the gesture acted to jerk the woman out of the trancelike state she had been in.

"And I'm Mrs. Donovan!" she snarled as she dragged her gaze away from the half-breed's face and replaced fear with distaste in her eyes as she looked him up and down. "And you're out of luck if you're after cash money. Because it's unnecessary for Barry and I to carry it. Why is it the poor always think the wealthy walk around with wads of bills about their persons?"

Donovan found his voice to order in a thick-with-fear tone: "Shut up, Eileen!" Then he cleared his throat and started to mash up the dead cigar in his hand as he told Edge in an almost squeaking voice: "She don't really mean to rile you, mister. I was broke for most of my life so I don't ever get high-falutin' about bein' rich. But Eileen's right. We don't ever carry much cash around. Usually we got on more jewelry, but on account of us bein' on our way to the funeral of an old buddy, it wasn't fittin' we should . . ."

He was sweating more profusely and his voice was getting thicker by the moment as the Winchester rifle swung slowly down from the half-breed's shoulder. Then he opened his hand to let fall the mess of the former cigar and began to try pulling off two rings that were trapped on his fingers by bulges of fat. His voice failed him again when the muzzle of the rifle was aimed at a midway point between the heads of the husband and wife. And Edge brought up his right hand to hold the barrel steady as he thumbed back the hammer.

"It's the truth," the woman pleaded, her former arrogance totally dispelled by a fresh assault of fear which this time bordered on terror. "We really are travelling to Prospect to attend the funeral of one of Barry's—"

"It's the truth I stopped the train to hear, ma'am," Edge cut in calmly across her fast spoken and shriller-by-the-word attempted explanation. "But only your husband can tell it so it'll carry conviction. Maybe his. And a couple of other fellers."

"I don't understand what you are talking about," Eileen Donovan protested, and shot an imploring glance at her husband.

He was once again dividing his nervous attention between the half-breed and the scene beyond the window. The sweat continued to ooze from his fleshy face and in rubbing at it with a bare hand he left fragments of tobacco and cigar paper adhered to the tacky skin.

"Figure he's getting to it, ma'am," Edge answered. "Having bad memories."

"I knew it," Donovan muttered, and now stared fixedly out of the window. "Frank gettin' shot down. The train gettin' stopped here. I want you to know before you kill me, too, mister, that I ain't gone unpunished for what we done that day to—''

"Mister, this ain't none of our business!" Clyde called croakily from the front of the car. "And I ain't about to allow my wife to be present when you cold-bloodedly—''

There was a shuffling of booted feet against the floor of the car and a rustle of clothing. Edge turned instinctively toward the scene of the activity, as Donovan started to cross himself. He glimpsed the woman with the baby in her arms being urged toward the leading door of the car by her husband, who was shielding her with his body. Clyde had not drawn the Remington from his holster. Then Edge heard Eileen Donovan's sharp intake of breath and sensed rather than saw the initial move of her attack—before he started to turn back toward her.

"Run, Barr!" she shrieked. "Get away from him!"

She powered up from the aisle seat, face no longer pretty as it was contorted by a mixture of anger and fear and hate. Both her hands were clawed as she reached for the rifle in Edge's grasp. And she achieved what she aimed for. Then, with a powerful lunge that allied physical capability with high emotion to produce amazing strength for such a slightly built woman, she shoved Edge into a backward stagger along the aisle.

For just part of a second after his wife was on her feet and driving the half-breed down the car,

Donovan seemed to be rooted to his seat. But then he lurched upright, staggered into the aisle and lumbered toward the rear end of the car, where he wrenched open the door, took two strides across the platform and leaped to the ground. He chose to leave the train on the Rock of Jesus side since there was no cover close by on the other side.

Edge had recovered from the surprise of the woman's attack by then, and had come to a rock-steady halt with his feet planted firmly on the floor of the car; the rifle still held in a double-handed grip across the front of his body where Eileen Donovan had forced it.

For several seconds after he became immovable, she attempted to wrench the Winchester from him. But the initial burst of energy she had expended to send him into retreat had drained her physically, and her emotional strength was badly depleted, too, so that when she at length allowed her unclawed hands to fall limply to her sides and turned her head to peer out of the window, just a single sob burst from deep within, this an acknowledgment of defeat as she saw her black-garbed husband moving at a waddling run across open ground between the train and the unfinished church—a clear and easy target for the man with the Winchester.

"You can tell the engineer he can move out the train any time he likes, feller," Edge said.

Eileen Donovan wrenched her head around and was in time to see the half-breed uncock the rifle and cant it to his shoulder as he turned from addressing Clyde, who was still on the threshold of the car's leading doorway.

"Dead men tell no tales nor truths, ma'am," Edge said to the perplexed woman. "You want to stay on the train and tell Prospect people they'd best put Frank Crowell in the ground without waiting for—"

"I'm going to remain with my husband!" she snapped, whirled with a rustle of petticoats beneath the skirt of her black mourning dress and strode resolutely along the aisle and out through the rear doorway of the car.

"You mean it, mister?" Clyde wanted to know anxiously from the front doorway as Edge went after the woman.

"Hardly ever say anything I don't mean, feller."

The young husband and father whirled out onto the platform and bellowed excitedly: "Hey, you guys! He says it's all right for us to leave! So let's get the hell away from here, okay?"

There was a chorus of answering voices from up alongside the locomotive and within the first day car, all of the responses incomprehensible to Edge as he stepped down from the rear platform of the second day car. Clyde was in a better position to make sense out of some of what was being shouted, and yelled back as the confusion of competing voices died down:

"No, nobody's been hurt! Couple of people scared all to hell got off the train! I got no idea what it's all about!"

Steam abruptly hissed out of valves with more

raucous force than at any time since the train came to its emergency halt. And against this sound, Edge murmured:

"An old mystery, feller. About ten Indians. Don't know if they were little. Just that now there are none."

Chapter Eleven

BARRY and Eileen Donovan were no longer running. He had ended his lumbering, fat man's dash near the diamond-shaped pattern of uninscribed grave markers, where he leaned forward from the waist and pressed his pudgy hands to his thick thighs, his head hanging down while he sucked in deep draughts of hot and dry air as he struggled to catch his breath and calm his panic. His wife was at first glance much more composed as she held herself almost rigidly erect—only her head moving, from side to side with an automatonlike motion.

After a first glance at the couple, Edge turned and dropped into a low squat; so that he was able to see beneath the train cars to where his gelding was contentedly foraging for scrub grass on the crest of a slight rise about a mile to the northeast. As he located the horse, pistons thudded and·drive shafts clanked, escaping steam hissed and wheelrims shrieked on the rails. The gelding interrupted his grazing, but then dipped his head to the grass again; horse sense telling him he was too far off to be in any danger.

Then the drive wheels found traction and the line of cars jerked forward and banged into each other with the force of momentum when the locomotive faltered from lack of steam pressure. But a stretched second later engine and cars were rolling in concert, the couplings that held them together pulled taut. And, as he rose from the crouch, the half-breed found his attention captured by the spotty-faced boy who was leaning out to the side from the rear platform of the first day car, a sneer twisting his mouthline as he yelled:

"At holdin' up trains, shithead, you ain't no Jesse James!"

Edge winced as he experienced twinges of pain from his hurried dismount, sparked by the crouch and coming erect from it. He murmured for his own ears: "Granted, kid. But he has some younger help."

The grim-faced brakeman hauled the boy in off the platform and Edge turned away from the departing train. First he saw Eileen Donovan, who was now fixed in a totally rigid stance as she stared back at him, the mix of fear and anger and hatred once again masking her pretty features with ugliness.

"You lying bastard!" she suddenly hurled at him, screaming it loud enough to be clearly heard above the snorting of the locomotive and clanking of the line of cars being drawn in back of Edge.

And the half-breed now realized the reason for the earlier mechanicallike jerking to and fro of her head, and what had caused her to voice an oath she quite obviously had seldom if ever used before— she had been switching her quizzical gaze between the portrait on the wanted flyer fixed to the telegraph pole and the man she now decided it depicted.

"It's you! You murdered Frank Crowell and now you're going to kill Barry!"

She whirled and clawed at the skirt of her mourning dress to lift it clear of the ground so that she was better able to run, but once more was transfixed by the unexpected. And Edge, too, was momentarily surprised by the sight of Barry Donovan.

The black-clad fat man had not moved from where he had halted at the end of his panicked bolt from the train. But he was standing upright now, the breath trapped inside his body as he pushed out both arms at shoulder level, his thick-fingered hands clawed, like he was attempting to ward off some ghostly apparition of his past evil that hovered above the eleven adobe grave markers. Then he swung awkwardly around, for a stretched second looking like a somnambulist while his arms remained reached out in front of him. But nobody could have stayed asleep during the kind of terrifying nightmare that was capable of inscribing the expression of stark horror which contorted the face of this man. Then he brought his arms down and began to run again, faster than before, and toward the train he had earlier fled from, a piercingly shrill scream venting from his gaping mouth.

His wife now lunged toward him, whatever she shouted masked by his scream of terror. Probably he did not see her and perhaps he was not even aware of her as she cannoned off his lumbering bulk and sprawled helplessly to the ground. Certainly he did not slow from his headlong pace, nor deviate from his elected course—which, if the train did not gather speed, would have gotten him to the side of the track in time to get a handhold on and swing aboard the rear platform of the caboose. But the train's speed was rising with every yard it traveled beneath the rolling billow of black wood-smoke that was stretched out along its full length.

"Barry!" Eileen Donovan shrieked from where she sat, splay-legged on the ground with both hands cupped to her mouth. "It's no use, Barry!"

Edge shifted his narrowed, glinting-eyed gaze from the despairing woman to where her husband now altered the direction of his run: Donovan unwilling to abandon the chase even though he had failed to intercept the train and the gap between the caboose and himself was widening by the part-second as he staggered along at the side of the track. Then he raked his gaze back toward the woman and past her, along the same arc, to look beyond the grave markers at the undoubtedly corporeal tableau that had triggered the fat man's massive terror.

Austin Henry Loring and Marsha Onslow walked side by side away from the base of the towering outcrop, the preacher looking no different from when Edge had last seen him—still unwashed and unshaven and attired in the ancient frock coat. He held his Bible open in both hands and appeared to be reading aloud from it. The woman with the blonde hair and statuesque frame was on his right, lightly holding his upper arm as if to steer him along a clear path while he was engrossed in religious study. She wore a high-necked, long-sleeved, low-hemmed dress that was gray in color and more functional than stylish, given form only by her shape. Her low-crowned, wide-brimmed hat was also undecorated by frills.

"Oh, God, his pills!" Eileen Donovan shrilled as Loring and Marsha Onslow reached the far side of the burial ground—close enough for Edge to be able to catch the mischievous wink that the woman directed at him.

His attention was yet again drawn to the fat man. And he was in time to see Barry Donovan weave on collapsing legs, trip on a tie and start to fall hard to the ground, his hands thrust out in front of him once more, but not in a pushing attitude nor in an attempt to break his fall. Instead, it was like he was making some crazed effort to catch hold of the caboose at the rear of the speeding train that was now more than a half mile away.

"I'm coming, my darling!" Eileen Donovan yelled. "I'll help you, Barry! Don't die, please don't die!"

Loring snapped his Bible closed and pulled free of Marsha's grip to stride fast among the grave markers in the wake of the distraught woman who was running toward where her husband lay ominously still after rolling onto his back. And then Edge moved toward the same objective, but with less haste, aware that Marsha Onslow was hurrying to join him. The bottle blonde fell in breathlessly alongside him as the redhead dropped hard to her knees beside her unmoving husband and shrieked:

"All right, you can forget it! Barry is dead! His heart finally gave out like they said it would if he didn't take it easier! So you've got what you want, you murdering bastard! Just as surely as if you had shot him dead!"

Marsha glanced at the half-breed's hard-set profile and was unable to see any outward sign of how he was reacting to Donovan's death by heart attack. She accused sardonically:

"You don't exactly have winning ways with women, Edge."

"Been known to beat them from time to time, lady."

"I bet you have," she countered, and there was a catch in her voice.

"It is another sign from the Almighty on high!" Loring declaimed, clutching the Bible to his narrow chest as he tilted back his head to turn his face to the naturally sculptured face high up on the outcrop of rock. "The second evildoer has perished by His hand on the very scene of his vicious iniquity! By this has God condoned what we are—"

"Shut up!" Eileen Donovan shrieked as she threw herself across the unfeeling corpse of her husband. "How dare you claim that the good Lord—"

"Vengeance is mine!" Austin Henry Loring interrupted the tearful woman in a tone of voice that suggested he was on the verge of venting triumphant laughter. "An eye for an eye! I am vindicated in my long-suppressed desire for revenge! It is already half complete!"

Now he fell to his knees, clasped his hands to either side of the Bible and bowed his head in reverent genuflection and silent prayer, while the new widow remained prostrate across the corpse, shaking with sobs. This as Marsha Onslow abruptly halted, only now aware that the half-breed had left her side—to step across the railroad track and head for where his chestnut gelding continued to graze on the crest of the low rise to the northeast.

"Edge!" she yelled, irritable.

"Yeah?"

"Maybe she knows something about the other two!"

"Not going anyplace I won't be coming back from, lady."

"You mind if I talk with her?" Marsha wanted to know, straining to control her ill-temper with the half-breed who did not look back at her as he moved toward his distant horse.

"Could be the kind that never gets done, lady."

"What?" she snapped.

"Woman's work."

"You are infuriating!"

"Talking."

Chapter Twelve

IT took the unhurrying half-breed something over forty-five minutes to walk out to where the chestnut gelding was calmly foraging on the hill crest, check him over for injury and ride him back to the late afternoon shadow of the rock outcrop beside the railroad track.

In this time, the train had gone from sight and there was just a faint smudge of dark smoke above the disintegrating heat haze in the south to show that it had disappeared in this direction; the sun had slid noticeably lower down the southwestern dome of the sky; and the group of three living people and one corpse that had been out in its full glare were now in the cooling shade of the Rock of Jesus.

Edge had watched the transportation of the body of Barry Donovan as he started to ride back—the remains loaded onto the rear seat of Loring's buggy that had been concealed beyond the southern end of the outcrop. The preacher had gone to bring the buggy to the side of the track and Marsha had driven it then, Loring and widow walking behind as if they were following a funeral cortege. The body was left in the buggy parked beside the chapel and the preacher appeared to be consoling the widow while the second woman started a fire in the circle of stones and set a pot of coffee to boil. There was a certain brusqueness about everything the Prospect woman did, like she was doing it reluctantly and in an ill-humor.

"According to your way of thinking, Edge," Marsha Onslow announced sourly as the half-breed swung out of his saddle on the other side of the track, "the preacherman is a real old woman! He's hardly stopped talking since you left!"

"The innocent should not be made to suffer, sir," Loring defended, "for the sins of those with who they have associated. This is certainly to be applied in the case of an innocent who until today had no knowledge of what took place here seven years ago?"

His tone and the expression on his skeletal face altered the statement to a query..

"Coffee's starting to smell good," Edge said as he led his horse carefully across the railbed, track and ties. And he appeared to be totally indifferent to the eager Loring, the irritable Marsha Onslow and the grief-stricken new widow, until he had hitched his reins to a wheel of the buggy and took his tin mug from his bedroll to bring to the fireside, where he dropped onto his haunches on the other side of Eileen Donovan from the preacher—the two of them seated on a block of adobe. And he said:

"You'll recall I made mention of why I stopped the train, ma'am?"

"I have no wish to discuss—" the widow with the pale, tear-stained face started to say, her voice unaffectedly refined again as she reached the numbed stage of coming to terms with grief.

"I said it was to hear the truth. Now your husband can't tell it me, I'm counting on you. There's no great rush, so I can spare you more than three. Even more than ten. Let's say a hundred, uh? Give or take a count or two either way? How about as long as it takes me to drink a cup of coffee?"

His tone was as neutral as his expression. But both Eileen Donovan and Austin Henry Loring listened to him and looked at him with mounting fear. The widow gasped and the preacher made a wet sound in his throat when Edge casually thrust his mug toward Marsha Onslow, who sat on another adobe block partway around the fire.

A smile replaced the frown on the face of the faded beauty with the bleach-blonde hair. And she said as she poured coffee from the pot into the mug and returned it to the half-breed: "Maybe you and he should switch collars, Edge. The way you have of putting the fear of God into people."

The coffee was too hot to drink at once. He rested the mug on the ground and took out the makings. He was aware that both the widow and the preacher wanted to speak, but could not trust their voices to be pitched at the desired tone yet.

"I ain't God, lady," he said to the Prospect woman.

"You know what I mean."

He sighed. "Yeah, I know."

"You want to know about me tying up with the preacherman and heading out here with him?" she asked, and poured herself some coffee in the mug Edge recognized as belonging to Austin Henry Loring.

"There's some coffee-drinking time to kill, lady. And women—"

"Yeah, women and talk go together like love and marriage," she cut in, ill-humor momentarily flaring in her eyes again. But when she glanced at Eileen Donovan it was with something akin to malicious envy rather than malevolence. But then she sighed, and peered into the fire with an attitude of resignation apparent in her expression and the posture she adopted on the block of adobe. "I never really did love Frank Crowell. I suspected it lots of times, but it wasn't until he was dead that I knew it for certain. Oh, I cried for him. But it was as much over my own feelings of guilt for going through the motions of grief as a bride to be; as it was for knowing Frank was down at the mortician's parlor and I'd never see him agin. You know what I mean, Edge?"

"Do I have to?" the half-breed asked as he lit the cigarette with a glowing stick from out the fire.

She was fleetingly sullen, then gave a slight

shrug and shifted her gaze from his face to study the heart of the fire again. "No, I guess somebody like you could never understand how a person can get trapped. Get into a nice easy rut. Know there's something better she can do with her life. But a lot worse, too. So she stays where she is, scared she might step out of the frying pan into the fire instead of the land of real living. And takes a drink or two over the usual on those times when she really gets to hating herself bad for not doing what she knows she ought to."

"Sister, you are speaking of the lives of almost every one of God's creatures who has the gift of free will," Loring assured. "We must make sacrifices to play our part in the order of things. Strong liquor is but a foolish palliative, my friend. Far better to turn to the comfort offered by the Almighty as we travel this vale of tears on our journey to His house of many mansions or to the sulphurous domain of the devil where—"

"Yeah, preacherman," Marsha Onslow cut in dully. "But when a person lives in a saloon at the other end of town from the church, liquor is quicker." She had looked from the fire to Loring and now glanced at Edge again before she returned to studying the flames and continued: "Anyway, I guess you've got the picture, mister. When you killed Frank, you made the decision for me. And maybe you did me a favor."

Eileen Donovan vented a strangled sound of shock and was ignored.

"Without knowing it, so I didn't figure I owed

you much. If anything. Except when you made it so I had to talk to you. But you didn't have to do that. You know it now. Frank Crowell's dead and gone and I can remember the good times we had together. While I take my chances at finding something better. And—sorry preacherman—without being much concerned if anybody up there is watching, I figure my chances will be better if I do what strikes me as the right thing. And, since I've good reason to believe everything the preacherman and you have told me, Edge, I felt I had to help the both of you.

"I started when I didn't snitch on you after you had the fight with Milton Rose last night, didn't I? Then, when I saw the sheriff and Mr. Loring putting their heads together in the law office I got to wondering if there was anything else I could do."

Austin Henry Loring had gradually sunk into a contemplative attitude that spread an expression of melancholy over his gaunt face: that was at the other end of the emotional range from the evangelical fervor that had previously lit his eyes and animated his sparse features.

"I apologize for not remaining where you told me, sir," he offered, in much the same flat tone of voice Marsha Onslow had used.

"No sweat, feller," Edge answered, conscious of the pale-skinned widow tensely studying his every move as he smoked the cigarette and sipped the coffee.

"But I got to thinking, you see. I know you

object to . . . to me preaching to you, as you infer it. But the fact remains, sir; in the darkness of the night I was visited by black thoughts about how you might interpret my agreement to you performing the will of God.''

"You came to Prospect, feller.''

"Yes. Yes. I don't know with what precise intention. Perhaps just a vague hope of meeting with you again before . . . in any event, I got to town very early this morning. Day was just breaking. Just Sheriff Milton Rose seemed to be up and about. He had me come into his office and began to tell me about the events of the night. Then Miss Onslow joined us. Since my mission now had the official backing of the law—man-made justice as well as . . .'' He cleared his throat. "Well, I was most anxious to confer with you again. In truth, to plead that you allow the law to take its course rather than to take it into your own hands . . . I'm sorry. It showed I had very little faith in your ability to exercise restraint, Mr. Edge.''

"Restraint?'' Eileen Donovan gasped in a strangled tone of incredulity. And she was ignored yet again.

"I didn't know what was going to happen, Edge,'' Marsha Onslow said quickly, fervid sincerity gleaming in her eyes. "But what I do know is the whole town's against you. Except for Milton Rose. And me. I figured that if I was seen to be on your side when something else bad happened, it would make Prospect people stop and think before they did anything they'd be sorry for.''

"Like lynch you," Loring put in, and produced a flicker of ice-cold anger in the narrowed eyes of the half-breed.

"And he's not talking because he likes to hear his own voice now," Marsha warned. "The sheriff's old and sick and he's not much more than a town retainer."

"He told me."

"Frank Crowell had a lot more respect. I didn't have any trouble at all starting the ball rolling and getting pledges for the three and a half thousand dollars to put up the reward. Part of salving my conscience . . ." She was momentarily shamefaced, but shrugged out of the mood. "Anyway, there's been lynch talk. And I let my conscience lead the way again. Rode with the preacherman out of town. Looking to find you. Went first to the place where Mr. Loring was supposed to wait. Saw somebody on horseback had been there and gone north along the railroad track. Figured it had to be you and so trailed you."

"We reached the Rock of Jesus while you were asleep," Loring put in when the woman paused for breath. "Needed some rest ourselves and so we bedded down without disturbing you."

"I wanted to let you know we were here," Marsha assured.

"I felt that here within the vicinity of the Rock of Jesus, the Lord's will would be done. As it was." He tilted his head to look up at the eroded top of the outcrop and smiled his contentment.

"It was the train stopping that woke us up,

Edge. You sure don't pussyfoot around when you make your mind up to something, do you? Holding up the train that way?''

"Orin stopped it with plenty of distance to spare.''

"I mean singlehanded. There might have been a whole bunch of hard men aboard. Any one of who might have shot you on sight.''

"Prospect ain't the kind of town hard men come to very often, lady. In a bunch or one at a time. And ordinary people don't take to killing lightly. Way Orin pulled out all the stops to keep from running me down with his locomotive, most men will hold back from using a gun against another man.''

Eileen Donovan seemed eager to say something, but Austin Henry Loring spoke first. Shook his head in admiration as he murmured:

"Foolishness and bravery are often one and the same thing.''

"With three and a half grand on my head, I figured risking my ass was worthwhile, lady,'' Edge said to Marsha Onslow. Then, as he tipped the dregs from his mug into the fire, he turned to the widow and waited for the hissing sound to finish before he asked of her: "You were going to say, lady?''

She shook her head much more vigorously than had the preacher. "No, nothing.''

Edge came erect and the suddenly breathless woman tilted back her head to gaze up at him. "Figure the count has to be two or three thousand past what I said, Mrs. Donovan. And in all that time you've said just the one word. That called into question my self-control as I recall?"

"You do not frighten me," she said hoarsely.

The negative action of the half-breed's head was almost imperceptible. But the woman seated below him saw it and she began to breathe as if an invisible claw had fastened around her throat.

"Bad start, lady. It's truth time, remember? And you're so afraid of me you're almost wetting your drawers."

He let go of his empty mug and it rattled on one of the stones encircling the fire and bounced to the ground. Both women and the preacher found their attention captured by the falling mug and each of them was startled by the sound of metal against rock. Then a far deeper degree of shock gripped each of them as Edge dropped into a crouch behind Eileen Donovan, forced her head back into his shoulder with the bar of his left forearm and with his right hand fisted around the handle of the straight razor, and pressed the side of its blade into the soft bulge of her cheek.

"Edge!" Loring and Marsha Onslow said in unison.

"It's the truth that I have no desire to cut you, Mrs. Donovan," the half-breed said softly into her ear that was partially obscured by her auburn hair. "It's also the truth that I will if you lie to me. Question: you knew what your husband and three other men did at this place seven years ago?"

She gulped and managed to force out: "No, I don't know what—"

"You knew he was once a friend of a man named Frank Crowell?"

"Yes." The gulp came after the reply this time.

"You knew Crowell owned a saloon in the town of Prospect?"

"Yes."

"You know of two other men who were close friends of your husband and Crowell in the War Between the States and for a time after it?"

"Yes."

"You know their names?"

"Yes."

"So tell me, lady."

"Please, you're hurting me."

"The truth often hurts."

"Maguire and Tremayne."

"You know where they are, Mrs. Donovan?"

Now she forced her head harder into his shoulder —so that she could stare defiantly up into his impassive face rather than in any attempt to draw back from the threat of the razor pressed against her flesh. "That was what I was going to tell you when you were bragging about you think you're the only man around here who can shoot to kill! You were lucky, that's all! Barry had them hold the train for as long as he could, but Maguire still ·missed it! He'll get you, though! Some other time! Especially when he finds out you've killed Barry as well as Frank Crowell! Maguire has a reputation as the most deadly gunfighter that ever . . . ."

She was unable to formulate an ending to the claim that she considered carried sufficient menace. And Edge filled the pause with:

"Ben Tremayne, Mrs. Donovan? In the event Maguire doesn't plan on showing up: because he's heard more about me than I have about him?"

"Please do not tempt providence, sir," Loring urged—like Marsha Onslow, less concerned for the safety of the widow since she had challenged the half-breed with defiance and not been made to suffer for it.

"How's that, feller?"

"To quote what is so often misquoted, my friend, pride goeth before destruction, and a haughty spirit before a fall."

"If a man can't take pride in the truth and in himself, what else is there?" Edge answered. And reminded: "Ben Tremayne, ma'am?"

"I don't know. I've heard Barry speak of him. When he spoke of Frank Crowell and John Maguire. Mostly about them all fighting in the war together. I swear to God, and you'll have to hurt me if you won't believe me, I know nothing about . . ." She ceased to press the back of her head against him and peer up into his face, to look imploringly at the other woman and the preacher then raked her gaze over the area of the outcrop, the chapel and the burial ground. Then she spoke in a tremulous whisper. "It is apparent to me that something terrible happened here some seven years ago. That involved Barry and his three comrades from the war. He never made mention of it to me."

"Obliged, ma'am," Edge said, and came up from the crouch, taking the razor carefully away from her cheek and sliding it back into the pouch at the nape of his neck.

"So you believe me?" She sounded drained and uncaring about his response.

"Maguire must have been someplace not far off if he planned to board the same train as you?"

"Albuquerque. It was purely by chance Barry knew he was in the territories. He never kept in contact with anybody he knew before he set up in the freight business in Santa Fe. He didn't even know Crowell was still operating the saloon in Prospect. He never knew where Tremayne went after the four of them went their separate ways. And knew of Maguire just from reading the newspaper accounts of his exploits. As fortune would have it, the man was last reported to be in Albuquerque. And when Barry received the wire from the Prospect peace officer telling him of Crowell's death, he sent one of his own. To Maguire care of the express office in Albuquerque relaying the same message. Maguire was still in the town and wired back that he hoped to join us on the train to Prospect."

Edge stooped to pick up his discarded mug and at the same time dropped his cigarette butt in the fire.

"What your husband and his three comrades in arms did here seven years ago, Mrs. Donovan—" Austin Henry Loring began.

But the widow raised her hands and pressed her

palms tightly to her ears. She implored: "I have no desire to know about it. Whatever it was, he has been paying for it ever since. By never experiencing a moment's peace of mind during his waking hours. And never once has he knowingly harmed any living creature or committed a single act of ill will against a fellow human being. And now he has suffered the ultimate penalty. Patently, he had a heart seizure. In a manner of speaking, that is what everyone dies from—the curtailment of the heart's beating. But I will believe until my own dying day that Barry died of fright. And I have no wish to know what magnitude of terror can haunt a man to that extent."

Edge had left the trio by the fire to go to where his horse was hitched to the buggy beside the chapel. He stowed his mug back in the center of his bedroll and then gave the gelding a drink of canteen water from his hat.

"Will you say as much in a court of law?" Marsha Onslow asked, sympathetic in her attitude toward the widow now that the earlier envy of her had been displaced by a degree of empathy—the bleached blonde perhaps wishing she was able to experience the same brand of loyalty to the memory of her dead man as did the redhead to her own.

"Opinions count for nothing," Eileen Donovan answered. "And if they were admitted in a courtroom, I would speak only good of my late husband. That is all I ever knew him to be."

"You're leaving, sir?" Austin Henry Loring asked anxiously as Edge put his damp hat back on his head and unhitched the reins from the buggy wheel.

"My business here is all done." He waved a hand at a fly that droned out from under the preacher's blanket that was draped over the bulky corpse of Barry Donovan on the rear seat of the buggy.

Marsha Onslow asked: "But you think there's a good chance Maguire will show up in Prospect?"

"That's my view."

Chapter Thirteen

THE man called Edge had not before noticed that the town of Prospect had a public clock that chimed the hours: until he rode down the north trail beside the railroad track among the homesteads and heard the three strikes that marked the time in the morning when, old wives tales had it, the human spirit was at its lowest ebb and the soul was most ready to leave the body.

The clock was on the façade of the railroad depot building, its white dial illuminated only by the light of the moon and the big and bright stars of Texas. This same light glinted on the dusty windows of the passenger cars and the polished metalwork of the locomotive of the train that stood silently alongside the depot boardwalk.

After the last echo of the chimes had faded there was just the clop of the gelding's hooves to keep the all-pervading silence at bay. And, as during his visit to Prospect last night, there was only a crack of lamplight to be glimpsed here and there among the buildings of the peacefully sleeping town. He reined the horse to a halt and listened fleetingly to the muted hum of a community at rest: struck a match on the butt of his holstered Colt and lit the cigarette that had been angled, unsmoked, from a side of his mouth for more than thirty minutes. Then he heeled his mount forward again as he blew out the flame. He toyed with the dead match between a thumb and two fingers as he moved his ice-blue eyes slowly back and forth between the narrowed lids. He listened as intently as he watched, while he relied on his sixth sense for lurking danger to warn him if a threat should suddenly manifest itself at his back.

It was obvious to anyone who witnessed his ride down the center of the main street that the half-breed was looking where he was going. Even more apparent was the fact that, although he made no more sound than was necessary, his approach to and ride into town was far from secretive. What the most diligent observer could never know was the extent of Edge's readiness to respond to any aggressive move against him by anyone tempted to attack him because they considered him ripe for ambush: for the stoical expression on his hat-brim-shadowed face and the easy way he sat his saddle was no more than a wafer-thin veneer designed to lure a potential enemy into reckless overconfidence.

It was a long ride from the railroad depot to Joel Slocum's livery stable, from one end of the street almost to the other: made to seem even longer by the strain of remaining tensed for lightning reaction to the initial sight or sound of actual danger, not imagined or innocent, like a seeming movement in the dark moonshadow of a sidewalk awning, the creak of a bedspring or the scurrying across a patch of moonlit ground of a mouse. Past the telegraph office and between stores and houses, the office of *The Prospect Tribune*, the Best in the West and then the stage line depot to his right. Over on his left was Avery's and Ruth's Aurora Restaurant. A few doors down on that side, a street cut off the main thoroughfare. Beyond this a dry-goods store opposite the law office. Then came the grade school and across the street from this the candy store and the barbering parlor with the alley between them where Frank Crowell had died.

Nobody threatened and nobody pleaded in the darkness of the alley tonight. The dog that had barked at him when he made his escape from town after he killed Crowell just whined now, as he rode past the feed and seed merchants, the two private houses and the boardinghouse of Mrs. Cloris Doyle. He swung to the right then, and tossed away the dead match, to ride onto the side street between the church and the livery. Only when he halted his mount out front of the stable and swung down from the saddle did he become aware of a sweet fragrance that competed with the acrid aroma of tobacco smoke for dominance of the cool night air. He had his attention briefly captured by a patch of color across the street—the floral tributes to the memory of Frank Crowell that were stacked on and around the mound of earth that marked the fresh grave in the cemetery at the rear of the church.

Then Edge dropped his part-smoked cigarette to the street and ground out its fire under a boot heel, opened the stable door and led his gelding inside to where the smells of horses and saddle soap and feed and horse apples and wet allowed no entry to other aromas. The stall in which his mount had previously been put was now occupied by another animal, so Edge put the gelding elsewhere—gave him a brisk rubdown and saw to it he had feed and water before he struck a match to check if there were any other strange horses in the livery.

Just the one—a big, powerful black stallion that was well cared for and had been resting here in Joel Slocum's stable for some time. The saddle and other gear had been taken by the rider to wherever he had elected to bed down. As he was careful to ensure that the match was totally cold before he dropped it to the straw-littered floor of the stable, Edge briefly pondered the possibility of the man sleeping peacefully in a room at the Best in the West or Mrs. Doyle's boardinghouse or someplace else in town. And was ninety-nine per cent sure that if the man who rode the black stallion to Prospect was easily asleep, the new-comer was not the one he had come here in the early hours of a new day to see—and had taken nerve-stretching and muscle-knotting precautions to be seen by.

He had been genuinely at ease while he was in the livery, but the moment he stepped out through the cracked-open door the familiar tension took an ice-cold grip on him in back of the impassiveness on his face and the nonchalance of his ambling gait. But the look on his angular features and the way he moved his lean frame was involuntarily habitual now—no part of any ploy to trick a wary watcher into a false sense of security. His right hand swung through a short arc that kept the slightly curved fingers always within a part of a second of fisting around the jutting butt of the holstered Frontier Colt, while his left was already fastened around the frame of the Winchester that was canted to his shoulder, thumb resting on the top of the hammer and forefinger curled to the trigger. Thus, he no longer simply invited an attack: he had set out to provoke one.

"You got nerve, mister, I'll say that for you!" a man called as Edge moved out onto the center of the main street again, where the side street between the livery and the church formed the intersection.

The speaker was some three hundred yards away as he broke the silence, and stepped off a shadowed sidewalk to move to the center of the same street out front of the telegraph office. But because of the stillness all around he did not have to raise his voice very much to carry what he said to where the half-breed came to an easy halt. Then noise, mostly of other voices, and an ever-increasing level of light began to spill from the buildings on either side, as drapes were jerked apart and some doors were pulled open. And the more impulsive citizens of Prospect stepped outside the safety of the buildings.

Then much of the sudden swell of sound was suddenly curtailed when the two men on the center of the street were seen. And the voice of just one of these men was again the sole disturbance in an otherwise almost palpable silence that pressed down on, in from the sides and along the street.

"Didn't expect nothin' less, though. After I heard tell how you stopped the train out in the boondocks. That was quite somethin', by all acounts."

"Don't they say small things please small minds, feller?" Edge answered.

The man tilted back his head and vented a raucous laugh as he started to advance slowly along the street toward the half-breed. "Lousy try, mister. Shows nerve of a different kind. But you can't rile a pro like me into drawin' against you over this kinda distance: you with a rifle and me with just a little old six-shooter. By the way, if you ain't already guessed it, I'm John Maguire. Old-time partner of Frank Crowell that I know you killed, and Barr Donovan that I reckon ain't in the land of the livin' no more?"

Maguire was pushing fifty and was no light-weight. He stood about five feet nine or ten inches tall and was broad-shouldered, barrel-chested and thick-waisted. He had a heavy-featured, ugly face with a thick-lipped mouth fronting crooked teeth, and small eyes. He was no longer called Red because the sparse hair on his shiny, domed head was gray. His eyebrows and busy moustache were gray also. Maguire's near baldness could be seen because he was hatless: he carried his Stetson hooked over his left hand. The hat was white with a black band. His shirt, vest, pants and boots were all black. So was his gunbelt. A silver watch chain was strung across the front of his vest and his dress spurs looked to be made of the same precious metal. His English Tranter .45 in a quick-draw holster was silver-plated and the bullets slotted into the loops of his gunbelt were polished so that they glinted in the light. Thus did the man look neat and clean, prosperous and dangerous: obviously was able to command top dollar for the jobs he undertook—and the fact that he was alive and well was proof that he always gave value for the money he was paid.

The half-breed who was unwashed and unshaven and attired in old and worn and unstylish clothes, appeared disreputable by contrast as he moved at the same unhurried pace as Maguire to close the gap.

But such a comparison did not occur to Edge, because he could feel no affinity with this man who was a professional killer. He knew that if this had been possible, he might have been able to experience a degree of respect for him: for the fact that he was here, doing a job out of a fraternal feeling from the past instead of for money; that he had not attempted to bushwhack his intended victim when the opportunity was presented to him; that he had shown himself to a man with a rifle when he was way outside handgun range; and that he was as tensely alert and ready to react as was Edge himself behind a front of casualness—this glimpsed in the way that his tiny eyes remained in a fixed gaze upon the half-breed when he had thrown back his head to vent the histrionic laugh.

"He died, feller."

"Dammit, mister, you didn't oughta have done that!" the tall and skinny and sickly-looking Milton Rose snarled as he stepped out of his unlit office, but remained at the side of the street. "You can't expect no protection from the law if you just go around killin' men like they was—"

A rising tide of vocal agreement with this sentiment drowned out the lawman's harshly spoken words. This as many more townspeople emerged from the cover of buildings along both sides of the main street; to flank the slowly narrowing gap between Edge and Maguire or to watch from behind them, everyone careful to stay out of the line of fire.

Maguire, still wary of the rifle canted to Edge's shoulder, did not look away from the taller, leaner man. While the half-breed, aware the Winchester meant he still had many yards to spare on his adversary in the open, glanced to left and to right; both ahead of him and then over each shoulder. He saw in passing as he searched without success for a sign that Maguire had an accomplice, that the sheriff was the only bystander fully dressed—everyone else was in nightclothes, some with topcoats draped over their shoulders.

The gunslinger with one hand hidden by his hat and the other hanging close to his fancy revolver vented another gust of harsh laughter across the falling level of angry words and then taunted: "You ain't gotta concern yourself with these folks, mister! Been talk of a necktie party, but that'll only come to pass if a saddletramp with nothin' goin' for him except nerve outdraws and outshoots the fastest gun from coast to coast, border to border."

Less than a hundred yards separated them now and they were not the only ones on the move. Many of the again-silent watchers were keeping pace with them; gathering into two close-knit groups, one on either side of the street. But the lengthening stretches of street in back of each man directly involved in the showdown remained clear: the tense-faced watchers wary of carelessly loosed bullets missing the intended targets to bore into equally vulnerable innocent victims.

"I knew I could talk them out of that lynchin' nonsense, Edge," Milton Rose assured, his tone less harsh and almost apologetic. He was moving along the street from the law office with that section of the crowd that kept level with the half-breed on the west side. "And I'd have gotten them to listen to me. Especially when they knew Marsha Onslow had left town to help you. But when the train pulled in without her or you or the Donovans on it, well . . . folks would only listen to—"

"Me, mister!" Maguire cut in eagerly on the lawman, who was again in danger of being shouted

down by his fellow citizens—the mere sound of
the gunslinger's voice enough to silence the crowd.
"It was my turn to talk the folks hereabouts out of
lynchin' you on sight, Edge! Told them how I'd
come here especially to pay back the man that
murdered my old buddy Frank Crowell. And how
I wanted to do it more than ever after I found out
he'd likely done away with another old partner of
mine. How it would be a pleasure for me and I
wouldn't want no reward for doin' it. Pleasure to
do and a happy memory to live with. Whereas
decent law-abidin' people, while they might get
one hell of a charge out of a lynch party . . . after
a time, they'd start to get a bad taste in their
mouths over what they'd done?"

He came to a halt and by both a change of tone
and an arching of his gray eyebrows he queried the
still-walking Edge for an opinion on what he had
said.

"I wouldn't know, feller," the half-breed answered. "I'm not decent people."

They were fifty yards apart and the gap was
closing more slowly now that just one of them was
moving. All the eager-for-vengeance watchers and
the subjugated lawman had shuffled to a halt at the
same time as Maguire, and a brittle silence was
suddenly clamped over the town. It was briefly shattered immediately after Edge's response: by a single chime from the depot clock as it struck a note
to mark the time of three-thirty. Several choked
cries of alarm sounded in the wake of the chime.
Then the unhurried footfalls of the half-breed be-

came the lone intruder in the tension-filled silence
that gripped Prospect again.

"Everyone knows that!" Maguire snarled, and
came close to shouting now that there was less
need than ever to raise his voice to be heard by a
man some twenty yards or so from where he stood.
And, just for a moment, a flicker of concern cracked
the contemptuous confidence with which the gunslinger had been imbued since he first announced
himself. Then, with a slight movement of his left
hand that caused his hat to turn, he recovered from
this brief experience with fear. Or perhaps, like
Edge, he was able to utilize such fear by control-
ling it and calling upon it to sharpen his wits and
add power to his reflexes. Whichever, there was
certainly no sign of apprehension in his attitude as
he now attempted to stir the fires of anger within a
man he obviously suddenly realized he had under-
estimated. And he sought with the carefully devel-
oped skill of a gunfighter to distract the attention
of his adversary away from his gun hand. "You're
a cold-blooded killer is what! Shootin' down decent people on the say-so of some hellfire preachin'
crazy man! A preachin' liar is what he is, saddletramp! And if you're too dumb to know that, I
reckon you're just too dumb to keep on livin'!"

After he had failed to get Edge to even glance
for part of a second at the turning hat, Maguire
sought to keep the glinting blue eyes trapped in a
fixed gaze upon his blazing green ones. "What'd
he tell you, Edge?" he ranted on, saliva spilling
from a side of this thick lips and spraying out

between his crooked teeth. "Not that he was in the business of runnin' liquor to the Injuns, I'll bet? Was buildin' a church that was really gonna be a storehouse for the stuff? Not that him and his two-dollar whore tried to keep me and my buddies back from the war busy while the Injuns was fixin' to do for us so they could rob us? But they was too liquored up to have a chance against me and Frank and Barr and Ben that had learned all the tricks in the book from fightin' in the war? Bet it wasn't nothin' like that the lyin' preacher told you? How we had to kill all them Injuns to keep from gettin' killed ourselves? Had to kill the whore for the same reason? Then tied him up to her carcass to teach him a lesson? And rode the hell away from there with him screamin' after us that he'd get free and one day find us and kill us all? I bet he didn't tell you none of that, uh? Or maybe he did but your kind don't give a damn why you kill decent people, long as the price is right?"

John Maguire asked the rhetorical question as Edge took a final pace and came to a halt about twenty feet away from the shorter and broader man. He timed the completion of this last step to match the thumbing back of the Winchester hammer, and answered as Maguire ceased to turn his hat and adopted the sideways-on pose of the gunfighter:

"Seems I'm going to have to kill you."

"Draw, then!" Maguire snarled.

Edge rasped: "I'd rather win."

Chapter Fourteen

IF the man facing Edge was not the fastest gun in the country, he came close. Even in the grip of fear and anger aroused within him by the icy calm of the half-breed, John Maguire's right hand moved with a quickness that almost deceived the eye to slide the silver-plated Tranter out of the cutaway holster. And Edge, as he spoke the sardonic comment, felt sure he was on the brink of taking a bullet in the heart. He could only will himself to continue what he had begun and ignore the end that was surely just a part of a second away: and resolve to stay alive long enough to blast a shot toward the man facing him—in the faint hope of seeing Maguire's lifeblood begin to spurt from a fatal wound.

Edge squeezed the trigger of the Winchester when the barrel of the rifle was just an inch or so away from his shoulder, knowing the bullet would explode harmlessly up into the Texas sky, but hopeful the report might act as some kind of hindering distraction to slow down Maguire, and gain time for himself to slide out of the holster the Frontier Colt, the butt of which was already in his fist.

He pulled back the revolver hammer with his right thumb as his left index finger triggered the rifle shot, and, an immeasurably short space of time later, heard a second shot. That should have belched a bullet from the muzzle of the Tranter that was aimed at him in the fist of Maguire. But the black hole at the end of the barrel remained cold and dark.

Not so a second black hole in the center of John Maguire's forehead an inch above the bridge of his nose. This one began to ooze warm and liquid crimson, as the leveled Tranter barrel was raked away from its aim at Edge—and the half-breed got his cocked Colt clear of the holster.

A chorus of angry voices was raised yet again along the main street of Prospect. But John Maguire was unable to shout against the barrage of sound to silence it this time. He was dead on his feet and starting to fall down backwards before he could swing the Tranter to aim it at the man who had shot him. The gun slipped from one hand and his hat fell off the other. Then, before the man became as inert as his Stetson and his handgun, Edge had both the Winchester and the Colt leveled at Sheriff Milton Rose—the spent shellcase ejected from the rifle still spinning in the air after the one-handed pumping of the action.

The lawman's Army Colt was not cocked as he

pushed it, smoke wisping from the muzzle, back into his holster. His teeth gleamed even whiter than usual in contrast with the dark color of his emaciated face as he looked down at the corpse with an expression that was held midway between a scowl and a grin.

The look that was fleetingly spread across the face of Edge when he first got his guns aimed at Rose was not dissimilar to this. And both men were for a stretched second as utterly unmoving as the corpse. And the sight of the three protagonists in fresh violence seemingly frozen in this statuelike tableau served to silence every angry voice and still the stir of movement that had rippled along both sides of the street.

"Glory be to Almighty God! His will has been done yet again!"

Just as there had been no need for John Maguire and Edge to shout at each other along the street, so Austin Henry Loring could have been plainly heard by everyone without raising his voice. But it was not the preacher's way to be reticent when extolling the virtue of his faith in good triumphing over evil, which he continued to do as he drove his buggy between the telegraph office and the train at the depot and headed down the street. He stood upright on the footboard with the reins in one hand his Bible in the other. He would doubtless have been ignored by everyone in town had it not been for the fact that Marsha Onslow sat on one end of the front seat and Eileen Donovan was on the other, one of the women recognized by Prospect citizens and the other by the passengers and crew off the train.

"I ain't much for honor, sheriff," Edge said, managing to keep his voice even-toned after shrinking his anger to an ice-cold ball in the pit of his stomach.

"If I hadn't sneaked out my gun to plug him, you'd be a dead man instead of him, mister," Milton Rose answered, dull-toned. He was peering up the street to where the buggy had been forced to a halt by the press of people crowding around it. And it was apparent the lawman would rather be in the crowd, yelling questions at the two women and hearing their answers—this interrogation having drowned out the preacher's eulogy on the alliance of right with might.

"Why I ain't much for it, feller," the half-breed allowed, and eased forward the hammers of both guns before he holstered one and canted the other to his shoulder. "But it still sticks in my craw that you—"

The tall and skinny lawman had seen and heard enough of what was happening around the buggy to be aware of a change of mood among his fellow citizens. And he curled two fingers and rapped them against his badge of office when he shifted his attention back to the half-breed and held the level gaze. He growled:

"I'm a small-town peace officer, Mr. Edge. Who never was as fast as Red Maguire even when I was in my prime as a Texas Ranger. But even if I was, this tin star and what it represents allows

me to do what I figure I have to so that law-abidin'
citizens are protected.'' He glanced to left and to
right. And so did Edge. He saw the beaming Loring
approaching from one side and the train passenger
named Clyde, without his wife and baby, closing
in on the other—looking nervous and dejected.
Rose sighed and went on: ''Though I have to tell
you, right up until I squeezed off that shot into
Maguire's head, I still wasn't sure I was killin' the
right man.''

''I know you told us to remain outside of town
until it was all over, my friend!'' the preacher
called, pressing the Bible to his chest with both
hands. ''But the women would not hear of it. Mrs.
Donovan has been totally won over to our cause
by Miss Onslow and they felt they had to try to
aid—''

''If you're still in any doubt, sheriff,'' Clyde cut
in, with an apologetic glance at Austin Henry
Loring, ''I reckon I can set your mind at rest about
that.''

''I ain't in no doubt no more, son,'' Milton
Rose answered, after he had peered up the street
again at the quietening, strangely melancholic, contrite crowd gathered around the buggy from which
the two women were being helped. ''But if I was,
why should I take any notice of what you tell
me?''

The fresh-faced young husband and father swallowed nervously and explained: ''My name is
Tremayne.''

''Well, I—'' Loring started.

"Not the Tremayne that was buddies with Crowell and—" Rose cut in.

"Clyde Tremayne, sheriff. Half-brother to Ben. Me and my wife and baby were at Ben's place when the telegraph from John Maguire was delivered to Ben's wife. Seems Ben used to talk a lot about his friendship with Crowell and Maguire and Donovan when they were in the war. His wife, she didn't feel up to attendin' another funeral, so she asked me if I'd come to Prospect and—"

"Another funeral?" Rose posed.

"Are you saying, my young friend, that your half-brother is . . .?"

"Yeah, reverend, Ben's dead. Him bein' buried was the reason me and my family was visitin' his place. He passed on after a long and painful sickness, which he figured, he told his wife while he was on his last, was given to him as a punishment for somethin' real bad he'd done years ago. He was ravin', his wife said, and she couldn't tell all of what he was sayin'. But it was somethin' about a bunch of redskins and a preacherman and a young woman. So from what I been hearin' . . ."

Clyde Tremayne shrugged his narrow shoulders and spread a quizzical look across his face, then sighed with relief when Milton Rose nodded his agreement with the implication. And Loring pressed the Bible tighter to his chest as he closed his eyes and moved his lips to mouth the words of a silent prayer. This as Edge dug the makings from his shirt pocket and began to roll a cigarette.

"Makes two of them dead from natural causes,"

announced the round-faced and rotund-framed man, who with his wife ran the Aurora Restaurant, from among the first shamefaced group of Prospect citizens to move away from the crowd at the stalled buggy.

"How's that, Avery?" Rose asked with a puzzled frown.

Avery jerked a thumb to indicate where the blanket-wrapped corpse was being carefully taken out of the buggy. "Seems that one had a heart seizure from overexertion."

"All you said was that he was dead!" the lawman growled at Edge, and emphasized it was a recrimination by directing a glinting-eyed glare at the impassive-faced man.

The half-breed struck a match on the stock of his rifle and lit the cigarette before he replied evenly: "I was a little too busy with other things to go into the details, feller."

He had difficulty in stifling a yawn and his eyes felt suddenly gritty with weariness. All around him, others showed signs of their own tiredness at this early morning hour after sleep had been interrupted by enervating violence—with the single exception of Austin Henry Loring, who intoned aloud in the wake of his tacit prayer:

"Sickness or the gun! The causes of the deaths of these four wretched and literally godforsaken evildoers may be disregarded as of little or no importance. The vengeance of the Lord was wreaked upon them, that is what it is vital to keep in mind.

And it is to be hoped that others who may feel lured toward the ways of evil will take heed of . . ."

He allowed the sentence to hang unfinished in the predawn coolness as the depot clock chimed the hour of four. And he became disconcertingly aware that he had just a single inattentive listener, since most people were returning to their beds while a few attended to the removal of the dead to the mortician's parlor, and a small group remained in sympathetic attendance on Eileen Donovan as she was steered by Marsha Onslow toward the Best in the West.

"You're getting the message at last, feller," Edge said absently, unconcerned that the guilt-ridden citizens of this Texas town were more discomfited by him than Loring.

"I'm afraid I don't understand, sir?"

"I don't want to be preached to," the half-breed reminded, and touched the brim of his hat as he made to move along the street, intent this time on reaching the boardinghouse of Mrs. Cloris Doyle without the need to shoot anyone on the way.

"You have my undying gratitude, sir!" the preacher called after him.

"No sweat, feller."

"The will of God would not have been done without you!"

"Reckon it's what us red-necks are here for."

"We are all here to—"

Edge murmured against Loring's sermonizing voice: "Help out you white-collar workers."

Watch for

THE MOVING CAGE

**next in the EDGE series
from Pinnacle Books**

coming in November!